ChangelingPress.com

Tobias/Justice Duet

Marteeka Karland

Tobias/Justice Duet
Marteeka Karland

All rights reserved.
Copyright ©2022 Marteeka Karland

ISBN: 978-1-60521-817-5
Publisher:
Changeling Press LLC
315 N. Centre St.
Martinsburg, WV 25404
ChangelingPress.com

Printed in the U.S.A.

Editor: Katriena Knights
Cover Artist: Marteeka Karland

The individual stories in this anthology have been previously released in E-Book format.

No part of this publication may be reproduced or shared by any electronic or mechanical means, including but not limited to reprinting, photocopying, or digital reproduction, without prior written permission from Changeling Press LLC.

This book contains sexually explicit scenes and adult language which some may find offensive and which is not appropriate for a young audience. Changeling Press books are for sale to adults, only, as defined by the laws of the country in which you made your purchase.

Table of Contents

Tobias (Salvation's Bane 7) 4
   Chapter One 5
   Chapter Two 16
   Chapter Three 26
   Chapter Four 39
   Chapter Five 52
   Chapter Six 66
   Chapter Seven 82
   Chapter Eight 99
Justice (Salvation's Bane MC 8) 106
   Chapter One 107
   Chapter Two 124
   Chapter Three 139
   Chapter Four 159
   Chapter Five 174
   Chapter Six 186
   Chapter Seven 198
   Chapter Eight 214
   Epilogue 228
Marteeka Karland 232
Changeling Press E-Books 233

Tobias (Salvation's Bane 7)
Marteeka Karland

Tobias: I hate bullies. Gymnastics moms are the worst, too. So when a girl who looks no older than the kids with the overbearing mothers steps in to take over, I'm more than a little skeptical. Her name is, of all things, Kitty, and I've been watching her from a distance. I just didn't realize she was a highly trained athlete in the body of a young, beguiling, innocent woman. Everything about her calls to my protective instincts. Especially when I find her putting herself in the hands of the very tormentor who broke my sister.

Kitty: Gymnastics has been my life as long as I can remember. Blowing out my knee just before the Olympic trials was not on my agenda, but here I am. The opportunity to audition for a troupe of renowned performers seems like a dream come true. Only it's a nightmare. Then *he* comes to my rescue. Tobias. He's scary looking, and so strong it takes my breath away. I'm crazy attracted to him, even though he's got more than a little violent streak in him. What's a girl to do? Me? I just roll with it. Until I can get him to claim me for his own.

Chapter One

One thing Tobias had decided over the last few weeks was that little girls ought to be able to be little girls. Oh, and gymnastics moms were bitches.

Like right now. There was a busty redhead yelling at a kid who looked like she was maybe in her late teens. Tall with flame-orange hair, the girl looked like she was on the verge of crying. Which pissed Tobias the fuck off. He wanted to punch the bitch in the face. Let her take a fall. Maybe she'd find out the fucking mat wasn't so fucking soft when she landed.

Just as he was about to intervene -- it was his Goddamned gym in the first fucking place -- another girl inserted herself between the two. This girl looked close to the same age. Slight of build, she carried herself with confidence. It was the only indication she might be older than a teenager. Her mahogany-colored hair was braided into a long, thick tail at the back of her head that fell almost to her hips. It was what gave her away.

Kitty was obviously very good with the kids, but she also seemed to be an accomplished gymnast on her own. Not much bigger than the orange-haired kid, she had more muscle in her legs and arms, though she was much shorter than the adult redhead. She talked to the older woman for a moment, smiling a megawatt smile, seeming to smooth things over. The older woman backed off, but shook her finger at the young girl once before turning back to the mothers' area.

Tobias watched as the two girls interacted for a while, Kitty obviously giving some pointers before putting a hand on the other girl's shoulder and urging her back to the large, square spring floor. Tobias had no idea how they kept everyone from slamming into each other, but each gymnast seemed to have his or her own section, depending on what they were working on. He watched for several minutes while the two girls went through some moves, then Kitty encouraged the other one to do the skill she'd previously fallen on. Immediately, Tobias could see how the stuff they'd worked on for a scant few minutes fit with the skill the kid was trying to learn. She stumbled a little on the landing, but she didn't fall on her face, and it was obvious she was pleased with the change.

The orange-haired kid jumped up and down, clapping her hands, and threw herself into Kitty's arms. They both laughed for a few seconds before the girl did the skill again. Then again. Repetition was a staple of gymnastics.

Not for the first time, he wondered why he'd taken on this responsibility. He'd volunteered to hire a decent coach and install the recommended equipment. Not high-end, but sturdy and competition legal. Three days a week, he opened the gym for the coach and her band of tumblers. They ranged in age from about five or six to high-school boys and girls. Classes were free to the students through level seven. Everything beyond that was preparation for elite-level gymnastics, which he knew from previous experience was basically Olympic level. Professionals. This coach said she didn't teach that level, and most of the kids were just that. Kids. Either in cheerleading or school gymnastics. Even though Salvation's Bane had discovered she was trying to break into elite gymnastics, they paid the coach for her time and gave her a decent, rent-free place for her students to train. In return, Bane used the place as a tax write-off and sometimes, occasionally, every once in a very little while, laundered money when they were paid for some paramilitary operation inside the US without permission. Happened from time to time when Thorn took jobs outside of ExFil, the security company run by the president of their sister club, Bones. Or something like that. Tobias didn't do tax shit. He punched things.

The reason Tobias had taken on this responsibility was twofold. First, he wanted control over the remodel of the building. He was the instructor for any police or military organization they trained, so he wanted a say in what it was OK to change. Second? Yeah. He *really* hated gymnastics moms. Always had. In his opinion, they were worse than Little League dads and pageant moms. They pushed these tiny little girls into doing things they could -- and often did -- hurt themselves doing. Tobias saw it as his mission in life to make sure any mom who was out-of-bounds got called out. Dads didn't seem to be as bad, but there were one or two. The come-to-Jesus meetings had been swift and eye opening for those men.

As he watched, the two girls continued until Kitty encouraged the younger one to continue on her own. Kitty gave a little wave and went to the balance beam and started working out, stretching and doing handstands and such on the narrow surface. The younger girl's mother, instead of praising the girl like Tobias thought she should, gestured wildly at her, obviously displeased about something. Fucking bitch.

Tobias made his way from his office to the stair on the balcony overlooking the massive gym. The place was three stories of open space. When he was training the guys, they built scale models on the floor to replicate urban settings or whatever they needed. Now, it was filled with local children on competitive gymnastics apparatus. He trotted down the stairs and stalked straight toward the orange-haired gymnast and her mother.

"Tobias." The warning came from the gallery where some of the parents waited for the lessons to be concluded. Stryker gave him an exasperated look. "You can't go beating up on women you don't like. It's bad for business."

"Ain't like we're gettin' money from this anyway. It's a fuckin' tax write-off."

"Yeah, but we still need it. I know you're headed to the redhead, and I'd say with good reason, but keep it down, OK? We don't want people afraid to come here."

"They yell at their kids like that, maybe they need to be afraid."

"Yeah, well, if you run them off, what happens then? Be nice so the kid has a safe place to go if she needs it."

Tobias sighed. He and Stryker always had each other's backs. But sometimes it was a bitch when Stryker was right.

"Fuckin' bitches are just as vicious as I remember." Tobias still stood there, watching. The mother seemed to sense his presence and glanced in his direction. Did a double take. Then she stood up straighter, her entire focus on Tobias, her daughter and the girl's perceived failure forgotten. She pushed her chest out and slinked his way.

"Yeah," Stryker chuckled, clapping him on the shoulder. "I hear ya. Good luck with that."

"Wait. You leaving?" It was all Tobias could do not to burst out in a maniacal laugh. It wasn't that he was afraid of the woman. More that he was afraid of what he'd do to the bitch if he had to be in her company more than a few seconds.

"Only stepped in to calm your tits. How you

proceed from here is all you, brother."

"Fucker."

As the woman approached him -- eyefucking the living hell out of him -- it took everything in Tobias not to take a step back away from her. The only thing making him stand his ground was his Marine pride. No gymnastic-mom bitch was making this Marine retreat.

"Hello there," she purred. Perfectly manicured nails reached for his chest. Before she could touch his shirt, however, Tobias caught her wrist. A not-so-subtle hint she shouldn't touch him. "I don't remember seeing you around. I'm Madonna." She glanced behind him, not making an effort to hide what she was doing. "Where'd your friend go?"

"None of your fuckin' business." Rude, but Tobias wasn't in the mood.

Red just shrugged. "His loss, but no matter." She gave him a carnivorous smile. "You're still here. We could…" She trailed off, her smile going even wider, "pass the time in private until my daughter's finished for the day. Could take a few hours."

It wasn't that the woman was unattractive. Quite the opposite. But she was overblown in a MILF kind of way. Obviously enhanced in several directions, with tons of makeup and not a hair out of place, she just screamed "fuck me hard." Normally, Tobias would be all over that shit, but the way she'd treated her kid was unacceptable and a complete buzzkill.

"Gym's only open for another two hours. And everyone has to be finished in one." He crossed his arms over his chest to keep from punching the bitch. "Orange-haired kid your daughter?"

Red scrunched up her nose. "Yes. I had hopes her hair would darken as she got older. We're going to have to dye it."

"She's just a kid. Don't yell at her like that again."

"If she's going to make it in Vegas, she has skills she needs to learn. If she's not putting forth the appropriate amount of effort to learn a skill, she needs to be encouraged to do so." Woman didn't bat an eyelash.

"Not in my fuckin' gym, lady. She got it just fine when the other girl worked with her. Maybe you ain't got the right teacher."

Finally, Red frowned at him. "I beg your pardon. I'll have you know she has the best coach in the region. Kitty's just a wannabe. Should have been in the last Olympics but couldn't make the cut. Might have made the first Tokyo team if she hadn't blown out her knee, but it's doubtful. Trust me when I tell you, that girl is nothing but bad luck."

"You seemed happy enough to let your daughter work with her this time. I'm bettin' you don't mind using her knowledge as long as you don't have to pay for it."

Red shrugged, not bothering to deny it. "Gymnastics is an expensive sport. We take free when we can get it."

"Like usin' my gym?" When she opened her mouth, but abruptly closed it again, Tobias continued. "Might wanna think about that. Gym's open to Coach Shannon three days a week. I don't ask no questions as long as she's in and out at the agreed-upon time. I don't fuck in her business or tell her who she can teach. That shit can change. I can -- and will -- ban you fuckin' gymnastics moms from the fuckin' building." He looked her up and down, putting the most disgusted look on his face he could. Didn't take much effort. "Bunch a fuckin' piranhas. Ain't seen a one of ya who deserve to have kids workin' as hard as they do to make you happy."

"Not all moms are like that." The second the words penetrated his brain, Tobias's body went tense, every cell straining for more of the lyrical sound. He glanced around him to find the voice. When he didn't immediately see the woman it belonged to, he did a wider sweep. Which was when he realized the only people close to him were fucking Madonna and... Kitty.

It took several seconds to compute what he was seeing. Sure, he'd seen her before, but always from a distance and always on some piece of equipment in the gym. Never this up close and personal. This girl was most decidedly a woman. It was her eyes that gave her away. Those eyes had seen more than her share of pain. This was a woman who'd grown up hard and fast. But she didn't look like she was much out of her teens. "Mrs. Scofield is just having a bad day. Besides, we worked through Julianna's problem. Another full practice, and she'll be more solid with her aerial walkover. She just needed a more powerful approach with a harder kick at the beginning."

"How old are you?" It was the last thing he expected to blurt out. Having said it, though, he was determined to get a fucking answer.

She shrugged. "Does it matter?"

"Yeah. It does. Coach Shannon assured me she was only teachin' high-school-aged kids. No professionals. You might barely be an adult, but you Goddamned sure ain't no fuckin' kid."

Kitty pursed her lips. On anyone else, he might have thought his vulgarity might have offended her, but, again, her eyes gave her away. And she was

- 11 -

laughing at him. "I'm nineteen. Definitely not a child, but I'm not a professional either. She isn't my coach. I just help out Coach Shannon when she can't be here. She has an elite athlete she has to evaluate for training today."

Tobias cocked his head. "She told me she don't coach professionals."

"Well, technically, I don't think this gymnast is a professional. She doesn't have sponsors, and she's only recently qualified as elite. She needs some help polishing herself for an elite coach."

"Still feels like a fuckin' lie." Tobias could really give two shits. He just wanted to see how Kitty responded. He couldn't wait for Glitter, Stryker's ol' lady, to meet her. She was gonna love Kitty.

"Either way, that athlete isn't going to work out here. Coach Shannon comes here strictly for level seven and below. And nobody pays her."

"What about you?"

"She agreed to pay me when I work in her gym, just not when I work here. The students don't pay me at all. No one pays me when I help here. It's for a good cause."

Tobias stiffened. "She don't pay you to help her here?"

"No. I volunteer to work here. Just like she does. It's not fair otherwise. Besides, letting me be here today the last hour the gym is open to audition to be Jackson Heart's partner is more than payment. He's only in town tonight and there's not really any other place for me to try out." Her eyes got wider. "Wait. Coach Shannon did OK this with you. Right? I know she said only students and parents were allowed inside, but this was supposed to be a one-time exception."

"There's got to be several places in Palm Beach

you could go. Why here?"

She sighed. "Look. It's just a few minutes. Thirty at most. He's coming as soon as the kids are gone, and we'll be out of here at the agreed-upon time. I just need the floor in case I fall. We've got mats, and the floor gives. I've never done this before so, if I fall, I won't get hurt." She shrugged. "At least, not too badly." He hadn't answered her question, but the girl didn't press him.

"Not too badly?" Tobias had to make a conscious effort not to step into her personal space and shake her.

"No. Won't be anything I can't handle. There's no jumping off a balance beam or swinging on the bars. No vaulting. Just two-person handstands. You know. One on top of the other. Maybe a few tosses, but my partner catches me. Any falls won't be more than six feet or so."

He sighed. "Whatever. Just make sure you're out by the agreed time. I have to set up for tomorrow." He didn't really like that someone he hadn't authorized was going to be in the gym, but with it set up for classes, no one could spy on their operation anyway. Besides, now that he knew about it, he could make sure to keep an extra eye on the security cameras. He sent a text off to Ripper, their intel guy, to keep a lookout until everyone left.

"I can stay and help. I don't mind."

Tobias smirked. "You stay here with me alone, you'll be helpin', all right."

"You don't want her helping." Fuck. Tobias had forgotten about Madonna. Probably because he'd wanted to forget her. She stepped into him, molding her body against him and scratching her bright red nails down his chest over his T-shirt. "She's just a little thing. I doubt she could do much to, uh, *help* a man like you." Madonna's voice was a throaty purr. Not likely. She was absolutely right about Kitty, though. She definitely wasn't his type of woman.

Bright hazel eyes with that wealth of dark brown hair he'd noticed since the first day she'd shown up. Up close, he noticed it was streaked with both black and blonde strands too fine and interspersed to be anything but natural. Sleek muscle bespoke long hours in the gym, but she was lithe instead of bulky. Not as filled out as he normally liked, but Tobias couldn't deny the appeal of her. Even if she was young as fuck. She looked like a little tabby cat. He'd like to see if he could make her purr like one.

"Besides," Madonna continued. "Julianna is auditioning for Jackson as well. I could kill some time."

Tobias gave Madonna an annoyed look. She was probably younger than him by several years. If Madonna's daughter was around fourteen or fifteen, that would probably make Madonna around thirty-six or -seven -- give or take. Which was still a good seven years younger than Tobias. But Kitty, at nineteen? Yeah. No way he was touching that. Literally or figuratively speaking.

"Madonna, you're already on my shit list because of the way you treated your daughter. Don't test me." He removed her hand and pushed her arm's length away from him before turning his attention back to Kitty. "And, much as I hate to agree with anything that woman says, she's right. What do you weigh? Ninety pounds? No way you could help me with the heavy equipment."

Kitty stiffened. "I'm stouter than I look. I help set up Coach Shannon's place all the time. If nothing else, I can help you move any of the gymnastics equipment if you need it out of the way. I know how it all sets up and is secured."

Tobias waved her away. "Just do what you gotta do. As long as you're outta here on time, I could give two shits."

Kitty flashed him a big smile. Which, in turn, made him want to groan. And double over in agony. That mouth of hers with those thick, red lips seemed to taunt him, and she hadn't done anything overtly sexy. Just smiled at him. She was young enough to be his fucking daughter, for crying out loud!

"Thanks so much, Mister…" She trailed off.

"Just call me Tobias," he said. "And make sure you let me know when you're out of here. I'll do a final sweep of the building and lock up."

Kitty's smile faltered for a scant moment before she turned it into a cocky grin and saluted him. "Aye, aye, sir!"

"Don't call me sir," he growled before stomping back up the stairs to await his invitation to hell. Because he was definitely going to be masturbating to fantasies involving little Miss Kitty's mouth.

Chapter Two

This was so much horse shit. Julianna was a good kid, she really was. But Kitty needed this gig with Jackson Heart. She'd only met him once, and he was a first-class prick, but the man was an ace performer in acrosport. Rumor had it his troupe would rival Cirque du Soleil if he kept it up. Now he was looking to replace his longtime partner after she suffered a career-ending injury the previous year, and Kitty wanted to be that replacement. Though Kitty had suffered her own injury, months of intensive rehab had helped her knee to heal. She wasn't a hundred percent, but she could do this. She hoped.

Kitty was good enough in every requirement and could add a new layer with her extensive tumbling and aerial skills if he gave her the chance. The problem was, Julianna could probably match her in most skills. True, she was pretty green and had no competition experience, but she was young and learned very quickly. It depended on what Mr. Heart wanted. If he wanted someone young and impressionable, someone to mold into the perfect partner, then Julianna had her beat hands down. If he wanted experience in both skills and performance, Kitty definitely had the edge.

But that wasn't even the biggest problem she had at the moment. Kitty had nowhere to live. Coach Shannon had promised her a small apartment above her gym, but that room was currently used to house the string of elite gymnasts she was polishing for a coaching friend of hers. There were at least five on the way in for eight weeks each, back-to-back. On top of that, the woman had neglected to pay her the agreed-upon amount for her to relocate. They'd opted instead for the apartment. Now that it wasn't available, Coach

Shannon hadn't yet worked out how she'd pay Kitty to relocate. If the woman had mentioned all this up front, Kitty would be safely back in Seattle instead of on the complete opposite corner of the country in Palm Springs, Florida. Instead, she was homeless. For the most part, she'd slept in Coach Shannon's gym. Occasionally, she'd found a nice place on the beach. Well. At least the weather was warm.

Her plan had been to lock up the gym, like Coach Shannon had instructed, but stay inside. She'd leave early the next morning before anyone got there. Of course now that plan was impossible.

Didn't matter. Right now, she had another twenty minutes before Heart arrived, and she needed to finish her warmup. Had she not stopped to help Julianna, she'd be on her normal schedule. Now she was behind, and it would mess with her headspace. She hated being rushed.

The balance beam was where she needed to focus. Mr. Heart would want her tumbling, but he'd test her balance and versatility in that area first. What contortions could she put her body into and still balance on the fewest points of contact? Most preferably, her head or one hand. She'd be expected to move with him, not just balance on the sturdy, if narrow, beam.

She did a back handspring into a handstand, moving to one hand, then shifting her legs into a different position. Then she moved back to the handstand before slowly lowering herself into a planche. It was a move where she lowered her body until it was parallel with the beam and with her arms in a nearly perpendicular line to both. It required not only balance, but raw strength. Slowly, carefully, so she didn't shift her weight too abruptly, she moved her center of gravity to one hand, holding the other arm out to the side for effect. She held it as long as she could before moving back to the handstand, turning and walking out of it so she was on her feet on the beam once again.

Then she did it again with a few variations designed to look impossible. She'd nearly gotten herself back into that comfortable place where only her body and whatever apparatus she was working on mattered. Her concentration was nearly complete, but there was that one little bit that refused to surrender to her will. Kitty kept hearing Julianna and Madonna arguing. Or, rather, Madonna yelling at her daughter while the girl whimpered and tried not to cry openly.

With a heavy sigh, Kitty jumped down from the beam and walked over to the pair. This had to stop. Not only was it getting on Kitty's last nerve, it was definitely not good for Julianna.

"Madonna, stop yelling at her, for Pete's sake. What's wrong now? How can I help?"

The older woman looked down her nose at Kitty in that superior way she had, as if Kitty were as insignificant as a fly.

"You can get Shannon in here! I'm calling Jackson. Julianna isn't ready, and Coach Shannon should be here. Not someone like *you*." She sneered the last word, as if Kitty were the worst sort of person.

"Coach Shannon gave strict instructions she was not to be disturbed. I'm not even sure I could get ahold of her if it was an emergency."

"I'm tired of your lame excuses! Now, call Shannon! And, for the love of God, call Jackson! I don't want him wasting his time when Julianna isn't ready today. I'm sure he can arrange another time."

"You need to calm down." Kitty was fast losing

her patience. She had as much riding on this as anyone, but that wasn't the problem. Mr. Heart was only in Palm Beach a few days. "This is the only day Mr. Heart had to audition anyone. We're lucky to get his time now."

Madonna snorted. "As if you had any chance at all. You're too old, and you're a has-been. He lost his last partner to an injury. Do you think he wants to take on someone who's already been injured? I mean, everyone said it's why you never tried out for the Olympic team, though I doubt you'd have managed to get to the trials. He's not going to risk losing someone so soon after he takes them on."

"That's up to him. In any case, Coach Shannon is the person who set this up. I'm filling in for her with the students, but I don't have her contacts."

"Filling in?" Madonna huffed. "If you'd been doing your job, Julianna would be ready when Jackson gets here. You've been too wrapped up in your own ambitions to properly prepare Julianna."

"I helped Julianna. If you'd bothered to bring her to practice on the days everyone is at Coach Shannon's gym, she would be ready. But you don't want to pay her gym fee. I didn't start my warmup until after classes were over and everyone was either leaving or playing on the equipment like they always do after class. But you're welcome to tell Coach anything you wish."

"Oh, rest assured, I will. You'll be looking for work when I'm done."

Kitty shrugged. "Whatever you need to do, Madonna. Just don't yell at Julianna. It hurts her, and she can't fight back. She'll never learn what she needs to if she's constantly worrying about whether or not you're going to yell at her for something she did an hour ago."

Madonna looked like she'd been about to fire off an angry retort when they heard a male voice headed in their direction.

"All I know is I've got two girls to audition. One is supposed to be good, the other teachable. I expect this to be a big waste of time, but I promised Sharon I'd give the one a good look."

"I've heard the girl with the knee injury has recovered nicely. Just not in time to prepare ready solid routines for the Olympics. Besides, she's a shade old for her first. Solid showman, though. There was a time when her coaches thought she had a legitimate shot at an All-Around medal."

"Yes, but that's competitive gymnastics. Elite gymnastics. I need a girl better able to put those skills with artistic gymnastics and combine it all with acrosport. If we can find that girl, we'll bust Vegas wide open."

When the two men walked into the gym area, Madonna immediately beelined to Jackson Heart.

"Jackson, darling." She greeted him with a hug and a kiss to both cheeks. "It's so wonderful to see you again." She motioned for Julianna to join her but never took her eyes off Jackson. "I don't believe you've met my daughter, Julianna, but I'm sure Shannon's talked to you about her extensively."

"Madonna, you're looking more beautiful than ever." Jackson's tone changed from the no-nonsense businessman skeptical of either female he was here to audition, to one of innuendo and familiarity. Yeah. He had other things on his mind with Madonna than auditioning her daughter. "I've heard so much about little Julianna here I feel like I know her already."

Great. Kitty wanted to barf. How many ways

could Coach Shannon screw her over? Why had she even brought her here? She wasn't paying her. She had assured her this audition would put her in a position to make use of her skills outside of elite gymnastics. All Kitty had to do was help her out a little when she couldn't be there, and help Julianna get ready for a move into level seven gymnastics. It looked like she'd set Kitty up to prepare Julianna for the job Kitty wanted. A disposable teacher who knew she had more riding on something than her boss did if she didn't pay her.

Jackson looked up then, and his gaze focused on Kitty. "You must be the girl Shannon said helped Julianna the past few weeks. I understand you have a wish to audition as well?" He looked bored, like Kitty was an afterthought. At best.

"Yes, Mr. Heart. I believe I could be an asset."

He looked her up and down like he might a car he considered buying. "Hmm... Well, there's something to work with, at least. I'll need to see what your skills are. I'm aware you had a knee injury that kept you out of the Olympic trials."

"It's fully healed now. I've completed very vigorous physical therapy. They put me through all the paces before clearing me to train. I've not had a moment's trouble with it since I started training again."

"Really? Then why not go back to elite gymnastics?" His raised eyebrow and the slight, sympathetic smirk seemed to mock her. Like he had her and there was no way for her to recover.

"At nineteen, I've passed my peak. I could probably have managed to get to the trials, but it would have been a waste of time for everyone. The coaches would never pick me at nineteen off an injury with no Olympic experience over a younger athlete with no injury. I had nothing to offer them even if I was good enough in one meet."

He nodded his head, looking surprised. "That's a very good assessment of the situation."

"I try to be realistic and honest, Mr. Heart."

He looked at Julianna. "Are you ready, young lady?"

Julianna giggled nervously, nodding her head as she glanced at her mother. Madonna frowned, and Julianna immediately sobered. "Yes, sir," she said softly. That seemed to please Jackson Heart greatly.

"Wonderful! Shall we begin?"

The workout was brutal. Both Heart and the man he'd brought with him -- no one bothered introducing him -- worked with her and Julianna. Kitty honestly couldn't say how it was going because she was so focused on just the next shift of her body weight she couldn't focus on anything else. When she worked with either of the two men, there was intense concentration. She was a new partner, and neither she nor the man she worked with knew what to expect from their partner.

Finally, Heart called for one last round. He led both her and Julianna in a series of balancing contortions and brought in the other man to be the second base for aerial throws. The last toss was a massive tumbling move. Julianna didn't complete the full triple rotation with the high flying aerial, but landed safely cradled in the arms of both men. When Kitty's turn came, Heart waved his partner off.

"I've got this. She did something like this for her vault. I won't be tossing her any higher than that, and she should have no difficulty landing it."

Kitty readied herself mentally. One base. One

catcher. No spotter. This was the real deal. He must think she was capable of this if he was pushing her this far. Kitty knew this spot was hers to lose. She tried to calm her breathing and get her racing heart back under control. She went through each move in her mind. She wouldn't ask if he intended to catch her. She knew by his words he didn't. He might steady her, ease her landing slightly by catching her around the waist with his hands, but it would be more of a guided landing than catching her in a cradle like they had Julianna.

Heart got into position and gave her a curt nod. Ready.

She cartwheeled onto his hands. Heart lifted her so she was in a handstand above his head. They moved to the one-handed stand, her legs apart, readying for the twisting flip that would land her on her feet above his head, balanced on his hands. The movement was flawless. Steady as a rock. As a base, he was solid. No shaking even when they were connected by only one hand.

Then it was time for the aerial move he wanted from her. Heart gave a soft count, then heaved her high into the air. Only he put a little spin on her she wasn't expecting. With no way to adjust mid-flight, her body registered the difference, and she popped the move, a reflexive protest of her body she couldn't prevent. Kitty went flying up into the air with no way to control the landing. In that second-and-a-half she was in the air, Kitty registered two things. First, she was fucked. Second, this was going to hurt like a mother bitch, no matter how she landed.

Sure enough, she landed hard, coming down on her knees. The worst possible situation for her. Immediately, she knew she was done. She had no idea how much damage she'd just done to the knee she'd worked so hard to rehabilitate, but it was probably extensive. And there was no way she got the spot in Heart's troupe. In fact, unless she was greatly mistaken, he'd put that little spin on his throw intentionally. Professionals of his caliber didn't make mistakes like that. Also, neither he nor his assistant made a move to help her to her feet.

"Oh, my," Heart said, tsking as if it were all just too bad. "You certainly had trouble spotting that landing." Kitty thought she heard a little titter from Madonna but couldn't be sure.

Julianna was the only one to come to her aid. The girl carefully helped Kitty to her feet. Julianna whimpered the whole time as if she were the one who was hurt.

"I'm so sorry, Kitty," she whispered. "So sorry."

"It's not your fault, honey," Kitty said between clenched teeth. She didn't want to stand, but had to make an effort. She might have made a fool of herself, but she had too much pride to just roll over and take it. She wasn't going to accuse Heart of throwing the move, either. That would be too much like sour grapes. "You be careful, Julianna," she murmured softly. Julianna nodded mutely, still keeping her arms around Kitty as they stood there.

"Well, I suppose that's that," Madonna said, a superior smile on her face. "Best of luck to you, Kitty dear. Come Julianna. Jackson and I have to discuss arrangements for settling you into his show."

"Right," Heart said. "Why don't you let Julianna go with Carter. You and I can discuss things much better on our own." The innuendo was clear.

"What the all-fired blue fuck just happened?" The bellow came from above them on the landing outside the offices in the gym. Above them, Tobias looked ready to do murder. In fact, he had a wicked-looking knife at his side, and he was stalking down the stairs.

Kitty knew she should be scared. Knew this wasn't a good man currently headed in their direction, but she was mesmerized by every single step he took. It was an exercise in barely controlled fury. The knife, the man, the muscles standing out beneath his shirt, the veins creeping up his arms, and the tattoos covering him all drew her attention, but the thing that fascinated her the most was his control. She knew about control. Recognized it everywhere she found it. This man was on the verge of a killing rage and was trying his best to rein it in. For now. And that, for some reason, struck her as sexy as *fuck*.

Chapter Three

Tobias saw her fall. Heard a little cry of pain. Then saw the two men standing over Kitty while Julianna crouched beside her, looking terrified. The fucking bitch, Madonna, looked almost gleeful. Tobias... saw red.

Snagging his hunting knife, he stormed out of the office and down the steps.

"What the all-fired blue fuck just happened?" He was keeping it together -- barely. The look on his face must have told the story of just how close to violence he was, because not only did the two men take a step back, Madonna tucked behind one of them. Julianna stayed with Kitty, and he noticed Kitty putting her arm around the girl in comfort.

Tobias went straight to Kitty, helping her the rest of the way to her feet. She gave a slight wince that was gone almost before he registered the discomfort, but she stood on her own, favoring her right leg. She kept hold of his shoulder, and he let her, putting himself between the girls and everyone else.

"I asked a fuckin' question."

"Slight mishap," one of them said. "She thought she was ready for the professional ranks, but she can't control her tricks yet. It was my mistake for not putting her through a more rigorous routine before trying the bigger aerial stunts." The voice was familiar, but the man had yet to turn around. When he did, a smug grin on his face, Tobias had to drop the knife in his hand to keep from burying it deep in the fucker's throat.

"I saw exactly what you did." Tobias tried hard to forget the brutal injury that had left his younger sister paralyzed, but it all came rushing back. "How the fuck did you get out of prison, and why in the

Goddamned hell are you back in acrosport?"

The man he'd singled out was now a sickly shade of gray, backing away from them all. He definitely wasn't smiling now.

"Now, everyone just stay calm," the other man said, hands going up in defense as he stepped slightly between Tobias and the man they called Jackson Heart. "I don't know who you think he is, but his name is Jackson Heart. He's never been in jail, and he's been in business with his troupe of aerialists for many years."

"I know all about his fuckin' troupe," Tobias spat. "My sister worked for the fucker until she was paralyzed. During a practice where she was fighting to keep her place in the show." He pointed at Jackson. "His name might be Jackson Heart now, but he was Sanfried Hammer six years ago."

The man straightened, dropping his hands. "I think you have him mixed up with someone else." He glanced over his shoulder at Jackson. "Surely."

"Well, he's scared shitless. And you ain't. Why else would he have reason to be that scared?"

"You are a big man, sir. And dangerous-looking." Tobias just glared at him. The man looked over his shoulder again. "Jackson? You're going to have to speak up here."

Jackson cleared his throat. "Don't know what the guy's talking about." His voice was high. Frightened. Tobias could smell fear, and it was rolling off Jackson in waves.

Tobias took a step forward and Jackson let out a yelp, turned, and fled the building. He turned his attention to the man left standing. "Who the fuck are you?"

"I'm Jackson's assistant, Tyger Wilson. Co-owner of Cirque America. I'm also a performer along with

Jackson."

"You have no idea what the fuck you got into, do you?" When Tyger only gave a little helpless shrug, Tobias growled. "Your best bet is to get out before he kills someone. I'm not sure how he ended up here or how Cirque Amerique is still around, but you should really ask your... *partner* a few questions."

"It's Cirque *America*," Tyger insisted.

Tobias shrugged. "Look up Cirque Amerique. Might enlighten you." Tobias turned to the two girls behind him. Well. One was a girl. Julianna was scared out of her mind. Tears streamed down her cheeks, which were red with both exertion and her crying. Kitty, on the other hand, was stoic as they came. The girl -- no, the *woman* -- had definitely taken her share of knocks. To be expected in gymnastics, but it didn't mean he liked it any better now than he did when his sister was in the sport. "Julianna, go with your mother. You don't feel safe, call me. I'll come get you." He handed the girl a card with the gym logo on it and a series of numbers. "You remember my name?"

"Tobias," she whispered as she nodded emphatically.

"Good. No questions. Day or night. Understand?"

"Yes, sir," she said softly.

"Kitty, can you make it upstairs to the office?"

She flashed him an annoyed look. "Been walking since I was a year old."

He got it. She was proud and didn't want those she viewed as her enemies to see her pain. He could also see her knee turning red even now. She'd have a hell of a bruise tomorrow.

"I want the two of you out of here," he said to Tyger and Madonna. "Don't come back. Julianna is welcomed anytime, but I better never seen either of you or that fucking bastard Jackson fuckin' Heart, or whatever his fuckin' name is, again. I do? I'll kill ya. Gators get hungry this time of year."

"Are you threatening me?" Madonna looked equal parts incensed and, unfortunately, turned on.

Tobias had to clench his jaw to hang on to his temper. He was usually better behaved than this, but seeing Kitty flying uncontrolled through the air had rattled him. "I'm holdin' on to my temper by a thread, lady. Get the fuck out. Now." He must have looked like he was ready to do murder, because Madonna put her hand to her throat defensively and gave a little gasp. She backed away before turning and walking away. It didn't skip Tobias's notice that she hadn't once looked for her daughter.

"I'm sorry to have bothered you," Tyger said with a nod. "I'll see Julianna is safe and make sure she has the means to call both of us if she needs help."

That surprised Tobias. This guy seemed genuine, but it was hard to tell, and Tobias already had preconceived notions about him given his association with that scum Sanfried Hammer. Jackson Heart. Whatever his fucking name was now.

He watched them leave, then took several deep, calming breaths before locking the door. He did his usual check of the building before pulling out his phone. Kitty needed a doc to look at her knee, so he called Blade, the club doctor. The man knew how to get in so there was no sense waiting on him. Time to get back to Kitty and see how bad the damage was.

Instead of the office where he'd expected to find her, however, she sat halfway up the stairs, her head in her hand and her right leg braced on the step below her so her knee was extended.

"Goddammit." He hated seeing her like this. She looked so defeated Tobias wanted to go back out to the parking lot, find that son of a bitch Heart and beat the motherfucker's head in. It reminded him too much of his sister. Only, at least Kitty was sitting up and talking. Walking. Kitty either didn't hear him or was too absorbed in her own pain to care because, when he reached the step below her, she started.

"I'm fine!" Her startled squeak and the way her hands went up defensively told a different story.

"Girl, you're anything but fine. Come here." Tobias bent and scooped up her slight weight into his arms. She cried out once when he jostled her leg, but otherwise stayed quiet. "I'm sorry. I know it hurts."

"I'm fine," she said again.

"Keep lyin' and I'll turn you over my knee. You ain't fine. You're hurt."

She gave him a glance, but kept quiet. The strain on her face said she was in too much pain to spar with him. Which just pissed him the fuck off. Kitty was used to getting hurt. Or at least hiding her pain. She just couldn't quite manage to get on top of this injury. Which likely meant it was bad indeed.

He sat her on the couch in his office, then went to get an ice compress and some elastic bandages, like Blade had instructed. When he came back, she was trying to swing her legs off the couch, presumably to stand up.

"What the fuck do you think you're doing?"

Her shoulders slumped. "Just trying to get up. I need to see how much damage I've done to it this time."

"That's Blade's job. He'll be here in a bit with some good pain meds."

"Really, Tobias. I'm good."

"Are not." He crossed his arms over his chest to wait for her to refute him, but she didn't. "What were you doin' with that fuckin' scumbag anyway?"

"Auditioning to be his partner in Cirque America. Guess that's out the window now."

"You probably just blew out your knee, and you're worried about a fuckin' audition?" Did this girl have no sense of self-preservation at all? She looked up at him, pain on her face. Unless he missed his guess, the sheen in her eyes had little to do with pain and more to do with whatever else was going on. "Tell me what the fuck you need that audition for?"

She gave a humorless laugh. "To live? I came here from Washington state because Coach Shannon promised me a job and a place to live. Bought me a one-way bus ticket here. She gave me the job. Unfortunately, she can't seem to afford to pay me. The elite gymnasts she's working out are living in the apartment I was supposed to have, so I'm homeless too. I have zero skills other than gymnastics. I didn't get to participate in the Olympic trials because of my injury, so I'm just another wannabe gymnastics instructor with no practical experience that says I can train elite-level gymnasts. I needed that gig!"

Was she kidding? "So? Get good at something else!"

"Says the person who owns the state-of-the-art gym and rents it out to the community for free three days a week. News flash, big guy. We ain't all rich."

"I don't own this place. I just run it." He scrubbed a hand over his face. "Look. One thing at a time, all right? Let Blade look at your knee when he gets here..." He trailed off. "Wait. If you don't have that apartment Shannon was talking about, where exactly have you been staying?"

She bit her lip. "Well, at her gym, mostly. Except she found me out yesterday. I was going to stay here tonight except you insisted on locking up yourself."

Tobias knew the second the words left her mouth, Kitty had had no intention of saying them. If it was possible for her to look any more miserable, she did. "I've got an extra room at my place," he told her. "You can crash there. I'm mostly at the club anyway. You'll basically have the place to yourself. Keep it clean for me, and you can stay as long as you like. Provided your knee is up to the task. If not, you can start once it is. You can stay there starting tonight."

"I can't do that," she said, shaking her head. "We don't know each other. I just met you! You know nothing about me. I could be a thief, and you could be a serial killer!"

"Girl, I got little patience as it is. You're testing the little I have. Your Coach Shannon gets paid for her work here. The idea was that she'd pull in kids from the community who couldn't afford her classes and teach them here. We pay her for that. So, while you're here helping these kids and she's off at her own gym working with world-class athletes, she's gettin' paid and makin' you fend for yourself." When her eyes widened and she sat up straighter, Tobias knew she realized she'd been played.

"But… but why would she do that? I'm nobody."

"How did she find you, Kitty?"

"She knew my coach. He helped me get this gig with her. Vouched for me. He said he wanted me to be able to use my talent. He said that, with Shannon's connections outside elite gymnastics, she'd be able to help me carve out a career followed by a strong base for teaching when I retired."

"First, you're not nobody. You're a highly

trained Olympic hopeful. True, you had no Olympic experience, but you've had all the training. You know what it takes to get there. You might not get top dollar to teach since you didn't make the trials, but you sure wouldn't get nothing. Second, you trust your coach to have your best interest at heart? I mean, you got hurt on his watch."

"My injury was just bad luck on my part. I didn't land squarely with both feet in a strong position on the beam before I pushed off for the dismount, then landed at an angle exactly on the spot where the mat was weak. Then, somehow, my ankle held but my knee gave way. Probably because I hadn't fully rotated due to the weak launch from the beam. I didn't get the height I usually get. Coach Don was there almost before I landed. He knew I was gonna hurt something and did his best to help me. He and his wife were the ones with me in the hospital and through my therapy. How do you know all that other stuff? What my experience is worth?"

"Later. Now, why didn't you call this Don when you got here and Shannon didn't deliver on what she promised?"

"He'd already done so much for me. I didn't want to burden him with this. My mom died right after I turned seventeen and Coach Don took me in. It wasn't like he didn't see me more than my mother did, anyway. Half the time I stayed at his house with a couple of the other girls who had single parents or depended on sponsors to pay for their training. He was always good to us and, as far as I knew, didn't milk anyone for extra money or anything. He genuinely wanted to work with us because he thought we had a future as elite gymnasts. Of that group, I'm the only one who didn't make the Olympic trials. All because of that injury. And he never gave up on me. I wasn't about to repay that with calling and whining to him that his friend screwed me over. He gave me a shot. I either make it or I don't, but I won't take advantage of his generosity."

Tobias nodded, rubbing his hand over his beard. "I can respect that. Also tells me everything I need to know about your character. I'm definitely settin' you up at my house. Don't worry about me. Like I said, I spend most of my time at the club. I'll make sure you're good, then leave you alone. Use it as long as you like. It'll just sit there empty if you don't."

She leaned back against the pillows he'd tucked behind her on the couch. "I guess I don't have any other options." She cocked her head. "Though, I could help you out here once I figure out how badly I've reinjured my knee. If you truly want a community gym for the city's youth who can't afford a gym like Coach Shannon's, I can help. I don't have the credentials she does with coaching, but I can teach basic gymnastics and introduce kids to the various apparatus. Not so much with the boys because they use different equipment, but everyone tumbles. And I can teach them stuff on vault. Maybe introduce them to the high bar."

Yeah. The girl was tough. He already knew she was good at teaching after watching her with little Julianna.

"Maybe this whole situation will work out for the best." He sat on the couch next to her, secured the ice to her knee with the elastic bandages he'd brought and handed her three ibuprofen and a bottle of water. "Here. Hopefully, this will take the edge off the pain before Blade gets here. He said he'd bring something stronger for pain."

"You don't have to do this. I can manage on my own."

"Yeah, well, indulge me. You seem like a good kid. Don't like seeing you in pain."

"I guess I don't have a better alternative. I've been here two weeks and pretty much depleted my cash. With no income, it's hard to stretch it much further."

"Give me a few days," Tobias said. "You get settled and rest your knee. We may be able to help each other, like you suggested. Have you had all her classes these last two weeks?"

"Yeah. Once I got here, she turned this gig over to me. I haven't done much other than spot and lead warmups. I've just been letting the kids tumble and play to get an idea of where each of them is at."

She reached up and touched his arm when he would have stood. "Tobias?" He grunted. "Thanks. You didn't have to help me now, and you didn't have to defend me earlier. I appreciate it."

Tobias just looked at her for a long moment, trying to gauge her reaction to what he had to tell her next. "You know, he intentionally threw that move."

She closed her eyes and gave a deep sigh. Yeah. She knew. "I thought so, but wasn't about to call out the man who's made millions in Vegas in his profession. If I'd accused him of a mistake like that, it would look like I was making excuses for my own failure." When she opened her eyes, she looked directly into his, and Tobias thought he might drown in their green-and-brown depths. A few ringlets of hair curled around her face having escaped the thickly bound bun she'd forced her hair into. Without thinking, he reached up and brushed one unruly curl off her cheek and tucked it behind her ear.

Her breath caught, and she gave a little gasp. She didn't shrink away but her pulse fluttered at her delicate throat. Even after he'd left her hair, the backs of his fingers grazed Kitty's cheek. It was the last thing he should have done. She was far too young for him, and he was far too fucked up. He had blood on his hands. Maybe not innocent blood, but the wrong blood. Perhaps the events of this evening had brought everything back. As excuses went, Tobias supposed that was a good one. Except the woman back then had been his sister. This woman was most definitely not. Still, everything protective inside him clambered to be free. He wanted to hurt. To kill. Kitty could just as easily be lying on the floor in a broken heap instead of sitting on his couch nursing a sore knee.

"You asked how I knew all that stuff about your experience. I know more than that. That man you know as Jackson Heart used to be called Sanfried Hammer. He owned a company called Cirque Amerique. That was six years ago, but he's not a man I'll ever forget. My sister was in much the same position you are, except she was auditioning to keep her position in his troupe. Sansa complained to me that her partner, a guy named Lucky Popolov, complained about her performance because she wouldn't sleep with him. Sansa's contract stipulated that she couldn't be replaced unless there was an audition, or challenge of some sort. It was basically the same thing you just went through. I only saw the last of it. Saw Sansa twisting in the air at an odd angle. She landed on the back of her neck and broke her T-four vertebrae. She's paralyzed from the chest down now."

Kitty sucked in a breath, reaching for his hand with both of hers. "I'm so sorry, Tobias. That had to be horrifying."

"About as horrifying as seeing you doing almost the same thing tonight." He brushed his thumb across the back of Kitty's hand unconsciously. When he realized what he was doing, he abruptly stopped, but couldn't make himself let go of her hand. "I'm telling you this so you know I know what I'm talking about. Sansa was younger than me by nine years. I practically raised her since our parents were older. She was twenty-one when this happened and had been in gymnastics all her life. She wasn't as advanced as you, but she went through some of the same training you did. I went through it right along with her. I was there at every single practice, every training session, every Emergency Room visit. So, trust me when I tell you, your man there missed that throw on purpose. He intentionally threw you off vertical so that you'd start your twist at an odd angle instead of controlling the movement yourself. Now, he can say that's the way he's always done it or whatever, but Julianna's throw wasn't off. Tyger was there to spot in case she missed her landing, but Heart intentionally put you out there to get hurt. I don't give a fuck what he says."

"I know," she said softly. "But knowing doesn't change what happened. It's always going to be his word against mine, and he's the famous one. I'm just the failed gymnast who got beaten by a twelve-year-old."

There was a long silence while they stared at each other. The longer he looked at Kitty, the more protective and attracted he became. Why? Tobias had no clue. He wanted to save her, but also wanted to redirect her path in life. He didn't want her hurt. And he didn't want any of his brothers getting ideas they could hunt her down for their own pleasure.

No. She was way too young for him. Way too

fucking young.

But the way she was looking at him now? The longing in her eyes? Maybe she needed a man like him to protect her. Even if it was just from himself.

Chapter Four

For several long, long moments, Kitty thought Tobias might be going to kiss her. Then there was a soft knock at the door and a huge, rough-looking guy stepped into the room. "Had to finish clinic," he growled. "Had a visit from Rycks and Shotgun."

"Black Reign?" Tobias got to his feet, not looking back at her, and the spell he'd woven around her was shattered. "What'er those fuckin' bastards doin' here?"

The other man shrugged and turned his attention to Kitty even as he spoke to Tobias. "Got into a bit of a scuffle. Not sure what the other guys looked like, but Rycks was in a bad way." He waved his hand at Kitty. "That her?"

"Yeah. Did what you said. Her knee's a deep red. Expect it'll be purple by mornin'. Kitty, this is Blade. He's the club's doc."

"You mind if I take a look?" He raised his eyebrows, but didn't make a move to unwrap her knee or touch her in any way.

"I guess," she said. "You're just gonna tell me I fucked it up again."

He snorted a laugh. "Well, I promise to soften the blow if you have."

Blade wore jeans and a worn T-shirt under a leather vest. When he turned to drag a chair over to the couch, she saw the vest had a gold-hooded skull emblazoned on the back. Above it read *Salvation's Bane*. Below it, *Palm Beach, FL*. Besides the obvious MC colors, his hair was a shaggy mess, and he looked like he hadn't shaved in a couple of weeks. His clothes and his hands were extremely clean, and he smelled like disinfecting soap when he sat next to her. Despite his gruff appearance, his touch was gentle as he carefully removed the elastic bandage Tobias had applied. The ice had melted somewhat in the bag, and Blade handed it to Tobias.

He moved her knee several different ways, asking her each time if it hurt. Surprisingly, the only time it hurt was when she bent it, and only at her knee cap.

"Congratulations," he said dryly. "I think you've broken your knee cap. Otherwise, I'm pretty sure your knee is intact. I'd like to get you to the hospital tonight to do an MRI, though." He reached for a bottle of water and handed it to her. She opened it automatically, thankful for a drink after the workout she'd just endured. When he handed her two pills, she took them, but didn't take them immediately. "It's painkillers," he said. "Percocet. Will probably knock you on your ass, but will help the pain."

"Really, I'm fine," Kitty said. No way could she afford that kind of imaging now. Hell, assuming she took Tobias at his word and this guy was actually a doctor, she couldn't even pay for the exam he'd just done. "The painkillers will be more than enough."

"Bullshit," Blade said without hesitation. "And I'm going on the assumption that you're either uninsured or underinsured instead of assuming you question my abilities. But you don't have to worry about that. We can do it off the books, and I'll get a colleague to read it."

"I don't like owing people," she said defensively. "I'm not a charity case."

Blade looked her up and down. "No. Definitely not a charity case." He crossed his arms over his chest. "You're a highly trained, intensely physical athlete. You've also had more than a few injuries, one on that same knee. You don't get on top of injuries immediately, your body will shut down. In ten or fifteen years you'll be lucky to be able to walk."

"I can't do this," she said, sitting up. Tobias promptly pushed her back down.

"Just lie there. I'll wrap your knee back up." He looked up at Blade. "What time do I need to have her there?"

"I said I wasn't going."

"Wait until about one in the morning. No one will be there. I'll call the MRI tech. He's been wanting to prospect for us. I'll dangle it out there in front of him if he'll come in and help me."

"You know Thorn don't do that shit. Besides, if it's Jason, he's too fuckin' young. Not to mention so skinny a stiff breeze would blow him away."

Blade shrugged. "I know that. Jason don't. Anyway, Jason's not what one would call a heavy lifter. Kid's a genius with mechanical shit, though. He sticks with it, he'll be prospecting with us."

Kitty was getting desperate. "Are you guys listening to me? I'm not going!"

Tobias grinned. "Baby, I'm a lot bigger than you. I reckon you'll do what I tell you to."

"Good," Blade said. "Now that that's settled, I'll see you later. I gotta check in with Vicious. Lucy's having problems."

That seemed to grab Tobias's attention. He sat up straighter, focusing on the other man. "She good?"

"Yeah. Just morning sickness.

"When it hit, it hit with a vengeance. I'm bettin' that young'un'll give her loads of trouble. This is God's way of not making her feel guilty when she has to paddle the kid's ass. Besides, she'll be fine in a few weeks. Until then, I'm keepin' a close eye on her. Makin' sure she stays hydrated."

Again, she tried to get up, but Tobias pushed her back. "Girl, you don't quit tryin' to get up and I'll paddle *your* ass. Sit. Still."

"You're crazy. I'm leaving. Thanks for the help, and thanks for looking at my knee."

"Where you think you're goin'?" She definitely had Tobias's full attention now. He waved absently at Blade. "See you tonight, brother."

"I'm leaving."

"And going where? No. You're coming with me like we agreed. Later tonight, we'll get that knee looked at like Blade said.

"I'm still not sure this is a good idea. You seem just a little too bossy for my tastes."

That got a chuckle out of him when she'd been deadly serious. "Honey, you ain't seen bossy. Give me a minute to lock up and we'll head out."

Ten minutes later, they were in a brand-new Ford Bronco headed west on highway ninety-eight. They turned off a couple more side roads and such before pulling into the driveway of a little house with white siding and a garage attached. It looked so… normal.

"Not what I was expecting," she muttered. She opened the door to get out.

"Stop." It was an order Tobias expected her to obey, if the tone of his voice was anything to go by. "I'll help you. And what exactly were you expecting?"

Thankfully, he got out of the vehicle before she had to answer, giving her a moment to form a reply.

When he lifted her into his arms, she tried to ignore how much she liked being there. This guy was not only out of her league physically, he was quite a bit older than her unless she missed her guess. He probably saw her as no more than a nuisance. At best,

- 42 -

she reminded him of his kid sister. He was a male in his prime. Obviously a warrior. Tall. Strong. All Alpha. What the hell would he do with a kid like her?

Nothing. That's what. And she needed to be interested in guys closer to her own age. Men who still had something to prove and made their own mistakes so she could be free to make hers.

"If you weren't expecting this to be my house, what exactly were you expecting?"

Yeah. Good question. "I don't know." She shrugged, trying to hold herself stiffly away from him. "Just something small and not so neat, I guess."

He grunted as he set her down carefully so he could unlock the door. He'd just scooped her up when three kids on bicycles wheeled into the driveway beside his Bronco.

"Woah, Tobias! Cool ride!"

"Sweet! Mike's gonna be so mad."

Tobias chuckled. "You tell Mike I flipped him off, will ya?"

"You said you'd get one before he did."

All three boys were talking at once as they stalked all around the vehicle. Tobias just stood there holding Kitty in his arms.

"Can we sit in it?" the smallest asked, an eager expression on his face.

"Give me a minute," Tobias answered. "Gotta get the girl settled, then I'll be out."

Three pairs of eyes focused on her curiously.

"Didn't know you had a daughter, Tobias. Mike never mentioned her."

"That's cause she ain't my kid, you little turd head. She's my..." He looked down at her as if puzzling out what her relationship to him was. Then he grinned wickedly. "She's my woman. You tell Mike

I got me a sweet woman who loves my Bronco. It's why she's with me in the first place. Tell him I said if he wasn't so cheap, he'd have himself a pretty young thing."

The boys roared with laughter and took off on their bikes. Kitty was so shocked, she couldn't say a word, just looked at him in horrified silence.

"What?" He chuckled, leaning in to kiss her nose. "You don't want to be associated with an old man like me?" He didn't look like it hurt his feelings.

"I -- I…" she stammered, not able to get her thoughts in gear. Because she really wasn't as offended as she should have been. In fact, her stomach had done the mother of all flip-flops when he'd looked at her, grinned, and declared her his. "Why would you do that? I'm not your girlfriend!" She wiggled, needing free of him. "Put me down!"

"Settle down," he said with a chuckle. "I was goading a friend and warning him off at the same time. While you're living in my house you will not date. Get me?"

She blinked several times. "No. I don't. My love life is none of your business. I could already have a boyfriend. What's wrong with you?" Now that the shock had worn off, she was getting more than a little angry.

"If you had a man, you wouldn't be at my house right now. You'd be at his. He ain't got a house? You don't need to be with him. And lastly, I'm a member of an MC. We do shit that's private. I don't want anyone thinkin' you're fair game to come in and start nosin' in my shit." He said it all matter-of-factly, not a hint of anger, but Kitty could tell he was serious.

"If I had any alternative I wouldn't be here, Tobias. I still don't understand why you can't just let me stay at the gym. Mats are pretty comfortable to sleep on."

He carried her to the leather sectional in the spacious living room and set her down gently, careful of her injured knee. "Because, on the days the community isn't using it, we use the gym to train paramilitary special forces. Trust me when I say you do *not* want to be around that bunch. They're rude and crass on the best of days, and any number of them would try to charm you out of your panties the first hour they were there."

"Well, if they're charming, maybe I'd like it if they tried." Instantly, Tobias shut down. His face went hard, and his easy-going manner vanished.

"You ain't ready for the kind of playin' those guys do. Don't think you are."

"Yet you told them I'm with you. Wouldn't that be like waving a red flag in front of them? I mean, my experience has been that men tend to want what another man has."

"Not around here. We respect each other too much for that bullshit."

"Still don't get why you care," she muttered, then reached for the wrap at her knee.

"Need to give it a rest for a while?" Despite his mood change, Tobias was as attentive as ever.

"Yeah. The ice has melted, and I could use a break." Once she had the bandage off, Tobias took the ice bag. She looked at her knee. It was starting to turn a nice dark purple on top, but other than the kneecap, it didn't seem to hurt unless she tried to bend it. She stood and put weight on it. No pain. She was beginning to think Blade had been correct. Maybe it was just her kneecap. It would seriously fuck with her mobility for several weeks, but it was something that could be overcome without surgery.

"You should really take it easy," Tobias said. He'd draped himself against the frame leading from the living room to the kitchen, his arms crossed over that massive chest of his. Kitty couldn't help but drink him in. He was rough around the edges and not at all the kind of man she should be interested in, but the way he'd come to her defense was definitely catnip to Kitty. She giggled at the analogy.

"What?"

"Nothing," she said hastily. Not touching that one. "I just wanted to get an idea of what I was facing. I think Blade might be right. Maybe it is just my kneecap."

"We'll know for sure after the MRI."

"Tobias, I can't afford that."

"This is old news, baby. Ain't revisitin' it. Just get some rest. You took the pills Blade gave you. Right?"

"Like I had a choice?"

"Should help you sleep."

"Yeah. I'm starting to get a little dizzy."

He flashed her a cocky grin. "Gettin' buzzed, are ya?"

"That shit always hits me hard."

"Probably 'cause you're just a little thing. That stuff's made for grown adults. Your body weight is little more than a child's."

Great. Just what she wanted to hear. "Well, I'm not a child." Why was she being so belligerent toward the guy? He was being a perfect gentleman. Just trying to help her out. Which might be the problem. Kitty wasn't a very sexual person. Or, at least, she'd never thought of herself as such. Probably because she'd been too focused on training to be overly interested in boys. Or men. Now? This guy was ticking every box she hadn't known existed for her. And, yeah, she was buzzed. Very buzzed. And getting buzz-ier by the minute.

"Can't argue that. But you're still a lightweight when it comes to the hard stuff," he chuckled. "Lay down. I'll get you up when it's time to meet Blade."

She didn't have the strength to argue.

* * *

What the fuck was he doing?

Tobias sat on the sectional with Kitty's head in his lap. He had no idea how he'd ended up in this position, but he had no desire to move. The woman had been in his life all of half a day and he was already infatuated with her.

When she'd passed out, he'd taken her hair down out of the tight bun and braid she'd fashioned it into. Thank God they weren't flying anywhere, because she'd set off every metal detector in the country courtesy of all the fucking bobby pins. Once he had it loosened, it was like a compulsion for him to brush it. He'd gone to Sansa's room and gotten the hairbrush he kept for her in case she decided to come back to live with him and brushed the impossibly long tresses for the next hour. The mass was thick and curly and had to hang past her hips. Definitely not typical for a gymnast. It must have been her rebellion. They all had at least one thing they refused to give up. Honestly, as long and heavy as it was, if she cut it now, she'd be off balance when she did anything.

Once he'd finished with her hair, he'd just sat there stroking it. The tactile movement seemed to soothe Kitty. She'd moan a little in her sleep every now and then. It wasn't a sound like she was in pain. Rather, she'd snuggle into his thigh, nodding her head until he started up again. If it was possible, a bond formed between him and her during that hour. Problem was, she was high, and he was fucked. He kept thinking about what he'd said on the spur of the moment meant as a joke on his friend. He'd said Kitty was his woman. At the time, he hadn't meant it. Not really. But now, he could definitely say there was no way another man was getting her. He hadn't been lying when he told her she wasn't to date while she was living in his house. At the time, he'd used the "club business" type of excuse. In retrospect, maybe he was already forming reasons to keep men away from her so he could have her for himself.

He'd been sitting like that, dozing occasionally, for the past three hours. It was time to get moving if they were going to get to the hospital to meet Blade.

"Baby," he said gently, continuing to stroke her hair. "Wake up for me. Can you do that?"

She moaned, stretching like a little kitten. No doubt, the girl was named perfectly. "Don' wanna."

Tobias smiled. "I know. But we need to go get those pictures of your knee. You can sleep on the way there if you want."

"Yeah," she said, yawning widely. "Sleep." Then promptly dozed off again.

With a soft chuckle and a shake of his head, Tobias pulled her into his lap, wrapping the blanket securely around her, and stood. She didn't so much as flinch. The sound of a Hog pulling up outside his house had Tobias frowning, wondering who it could be. Just as Tobias got to the door, Blade opened it.

"What the hell're you doin' here? Ain't we supposed to meet you at the hospital?"

"Yeah." Blade grinned at him. "I take it the Percocet hit her hard."

"You could say that." Kitty's head lolled against

his shoulder, and there was a little drool coming from the corner of her mouth. At any other time in his life, it would have annoyed him. Now, he just chuckled softly.

"Figured. I just stopped on my way to see if you needed help getting her there."

"It'd be good if you could help me get her in the Bronco."

Together, they easily got her settled with her seat belt securely fastened and the blanket snug around her. Blade got back on his Harley and sped off. The sound of the rattling pipes woke Kitty with a start.

"Wha --?"

"Shh, baby. Relax. We're just headed to the hospital. Remember?"

"I thought I told you I wasn't going?" That little frown of hers turned him on for some reason. Probably because he knew it meant she was going to spar with him.

He shrugged. "You did. I overruled you."

"You don't get to overrule me. I'm an adult."

"Yup. But you're my woman. Remember?" Goading her was going to be so much fun. Her eyes widened, all traces of sleep vanishing in a millisecond.

"I am *not* your woman."

"Oh, yeah? Ask Mike. He's been tellin' everyone he can find I've gotten myself hitched."

"That sounds like a you problem."

"It definitely is. Unfortunately, I'm making it a you problem, too."

She gave a frustrated growl, shaking her head as if to clear it. Probably still buzzing. Or hungover. Either one would work to his advantage. "I can't do this with you right now."

"Good. Just sit back and close your eyes. We'll be

there in ten."

Kitty gave him surprisingly little trouble from then until they finally pulled back into the driveway at three in the morning. She continued to doze and probably would for several more hours. Blade had given her a shot of something "good," and it had hit much faster than the Percocet from earlier. She was out like a light.

When he got her inside, he debated putting her in Sansa's bed, but decided against it. For one, that was Sansa's room. While he didn't mind letting someone else use it, he didn't want it to be occupied if his sister suddenly called and decided to come home instead of staying in the nursing facility she'd been at for the last six years. Long shot, but there it was. Instead, he put Kitty in his bed. Seeing her there in the middle of the big king-size bed made him instantly hard. She was a beautiful woman. All lean muscle and lithe grace. But he could never have her. Not really. At least, not like this. And certainly not until she had her wits about her. But he was a bad-ass-looking male in his prime. Women routinely fell at his feet, knowing exactly what they were getting when they hooked up with him. He'd be rough, but he'd give as good as he got. He wasn't so sure little Kitty was up for his brand of sex. Yet.

He could get her there, he was sure of it. The only question was if it was worth the trouble. She had demons that needed slaying and his sister needed avenging. Once he took care of Sanfried Hammer, aka Jackson Heart, she probably wouldn't want to even look at him again.

A problem for another time. Right now, he stripped down to his boxers and climbed into bed with her. With all that medication on board, he needed to keep a close eye on her. As he pulled her into his arms and she snuggled against him, he grinned. Yeah. This was why he was in his bed with her. Definitely to keep an eye on her.

Chapter Five

The most wonderful scent surrounded Kitty, all masculine and comforting. She snuggled into the pillow, reaching out beside her, fully expecting to find a man in her bed. Maybe that rugged, tough man from her dreams who'd saved her and taken care of her. No. That was nothing more than a dream. At least she'd hoped it was. Otherwise, she was looking at another knee injury and no means of supporting herself.

She curled her knees up into a position of comfort so she could drift off. Maybe float back into that delicious dream. Reality hit her with the force of a broken kneecap when she bent her right leg. Holding back the cry wasn't even possible. She'd been so sleep-fogged her defenses were completely down.

"Oh, God," she moaned. "This can't be happening. This *can't* be happening!"

She was trying her best to get out of the bed -- a bed she suddenly realized wasn't hers -- when the door opened and the room seemed to fill with that clean, comforting, masculine smell she'd woken to.

"Hey, take it easy," he said. A big hand pressed on her shoulder, urging her to lie back down. Kitty thought she had to obey that big hand because the pain was so unexpected. As long as she didn't move, her knee just ached. Move it and pain seemed to explode all around her. "Blade brought a knee brace for you if you had trouble. Said you didn't necessarily need it, but it would help remind you to keep your knee straightened."

"This is really happening, isn't it?" Kitty was starting to feel desperate. "Everything from yesterday. Last night." She looked up at the man, whose scent haunted her dreams in the sweetest of ways. The rugged man who'd saved her from a bad situation, brought in help to take care of her when she'd hurt her knee, and had apparently watched over her all night.

"What's happening? You got hurt, if that's what you mean. But it's not all that horrible."

"Not horrible?" She wanted to cry. Not so much with the pain. She'd been through that before. But with frustration. How was she going to work in Cirque America if her knee was hurt? Then she remembered *how* she hurt her knee and tears truly did come. "Goddammit!"

"Here," Tobias handed her a glass of water and two pills. "This will help the pain."

She shook her head, trying to push the water away. "I've had too much of that stuff already. It makes my head fuzzy."

"I know. Fortunately you don't need your wits about you right now. Now, take the pills while I put the brace on your knee, and then I'll help you to the bathroom. After that, I can take you to the couch if you like. You can kick back and watch TV."

"This is so fucked up," she said, taking the water and pills from him because, really, what was the point of postponing the inevitable? She was hurting. The pain wasn't going away for a few weeks, and all she was doing by refusing to take the medicine was suffering needlessly. "I've got to find a fucking job," she muttered.

Tobias tilted his head at her, giving her a strange look. "Don't you remember anything about the conversation yesterday?"

Her gaze snapped to his. What had she forgotten? Was it important? Judging by the puzzled look on his face, it was important. Helplessly, she shook her head.

"You're taking over the work with community children three days a week. You've been doing it for the last two weeks anyway. Only, now, you're getting paid for it."

Her eyes widened. Oh, yeah. Well, shit. "How much am I making?"

He chuckled. "We hadn't discussed it, but we're giving Coach Shannon three thousand a month. That was supposed to be for her time with the kids and for planning events. In the year she's been doing this for us, she's not had any meets or recitals or whatever. Just gymnastics three days a week. She taught them, but she didn't provide the means for them to increase their individual level. If you agree to at least try to put something like that together for these kids, I'll see to it you get a salary increase as well as a separate budget."

For a moment, Kitty just looked at him. This didn't compute. At all.

"Well? You still game? It's not a whole lot, but it's an opportunity for you to not only build a client base, but to help the community. You can run it any way you want, but you can't take money from the kids for lessons, and we prefer it be to kids who wouldn't otherwise have this opportunity."

Then she pounced. "You swear I can I run it the way I want?"

"Absolutely. You tell me what you need and it's yours."

"If you're pranking me, Tobias…"

"Not at all, honey. We thought we had a good fit with Shannon, but we were obviously wrong. You're familiar with the kids and what we're trying to do, so we'll put it in your capable hands. I talked with Thorn last night and, once we put it to a vote, it will be official."

"Who's that?"

"Thorn's our president. Do you remember anything from last night?"

She sighed, probably looking more than a little disgruntled. "It's coming back as we talk. The gym is owned by Salvation's Bane. Right?"

"Yeah. Thorn is the president of Bane. Ultimately he makes the decisions, but we all get a vote. Trust me. You're in. Already got the background check from our sister club, so you're good."

"I'll have to be ready by Monday," she mused, her mind already turning. "So much to plan. We need to advertise. There aren't nearly enough kids coming through now to make an impact. We need fundraisers and advertising…"

Tobias chuckled. "One thing at a time, little girl. Today is rest mode. You want to jot down some ideas, that's fine. But you're not working. You're resting."

"Who has time for rest?" Just thinking about the amount of work she was going to have to put into this was already making her head spin. "I'm basically taking over a business with no information about it! Holy hell! I'll have to get the information from Coach Shannon." She froze. "Oh, shit." Her gaze darted to Tobias's. "She's not gonna be happy losing three thousand a month, is she?"

"Likely not. But don't worry about that. There's two weeks until the end of the month, when she gets paid. Let her know you injured your knee and aren't available for classes the next two weeks. I'll take care of the rest. You'll start first of the month, and I'll make sure you get half the first month's salary up front."

"That leaves me two weeks before I have a way to support myself." She'd just been musing that last bit out loud, but quickly added, "I'm not complaining. I appreciate all you've done."

"Honey, don't worry about it. I've got you until then. You just rest your knee and think about what you want to do with the gym."

He helped her to her feet, letting her half-walk to the bathroom while he supported her. "I need a bath," she said. "I didn't take one last night, and I'm sure I stink."

"Just good clean sweat." He winked at her. "Wash off if you need to. We'll see about a shower later tonight."

She looked up at him. "You seem far too accepting of this. I'd have thought having an invalid in your house would be inconvenient for you."

"Not when the invalid in question is such a pretty little thing. Besides, I think word's gotten around I have a woman, thanks to that bastard Mike."

"If the grin on your face is anything to go by, you're not as upset as you should be. Not that you don't deserve it. You brought it all on yourself."

"Honey, I've got a woman nearly twenty years younger than me. What's not to love about that?"

She snorted. "Well, you can just think again. I'm not your woman."

"Yet."

If the conversation hadn't been so absurd, she'd have screeched at him in frustration. Instead, she just shook her head. "You're crazy."

"So I've been told, but then, so is every single member of Salvation's Bane. Don't be gettin' any ideas, though. You're all for me." The smile he gave her was positively wicked.

God, she wanted that to be true! Did the hope she felt blossoming in her chest show on her face? She hoped not. Kitty hadn't even known Tobias twenty-four hours. Sure, she'd seen him at the gym. He ran the place, for crying out loud. No way to miss him. But she'd always thought he was unattainable. Good eye candy, dream fantasies, and masturbation material, but not a man she'd ever experience in all his carnal delights.

The next two weeks were so surreal Kitty had to constantly remind herself she was, indeed, awake and not in some kind of weird, kinky dream where she tortured herself daily with thoughts of the sexy man she was living with. He'd told her he wouldn't be at the house much, that he spent most of his time at the club. While several members of Salvation's Bane dropped by the house daily, Tobias seemed to always be home. More, he always seemed to be in her shit. At least, he seemed to actively look for ways to be right where she was. Usually, he was fussing over her knee. Always, he flirted outrageously with her, making her question whether or not he was serious about taking her to bed once her knee had healed enough.

Like now. He was leaning against the bathroom vanity while she tried to cover herself with a washcloth and bubbles.

"What the hell are you doing? Get out!"

"Enjoyin' the view too much to leave, darlin'," he drawled. He shook his head in that way men did when they appreciated what they were looking at. "I definitely chose well. Can't wait to get to explore that tight little body of yours up close and personal."

"Who said that was happening?" He kept it up, and it was totally happening. Besides the fact Kitty absolutely loved that raspy voice he had, no one had ever made her feel this desirable. Admittedly, she'd been way too engrossed in her training to interact with anyone not in her gym, but it was still a heady experience. Over the last two weeks she'd been the center of his attention, and she was rapidly growing addicted.

"Oh, baby. It's happening. It's just a matter of when." He winked at her, straightening and sauntering over to her. "You'll be ready soon. When you are, we're gonna have a hell of a time."

Kitty swallowed. Oh, God. She believed him. "I-I don't know about this."

"My advice is to just go with it." He squatted down, looking into the water. Dipping his finger in, he made lazy circles in the bubbles. "How's your knee?" The question was asked casually. In fact, he'd asked her that every day since that first night.

"Better," she croaked. She couldn't think with him this close. Hell. Her body had erupted in sweat and she was trembling, on fire with a sudden need she didn't clearly understand. "Better than I thought it would be only two weeks in."

"Still sore when you bend it?"

"A bit."

He grinned at her, standing and holding a hand out to her.

"What?" She looked from him to his hand in confusion.

"Out of the tub. You'll turn into a prune."

She blinked up at him. "I'm not getting out with you standing there. I'm naked!"

"Usually happens when you take a bath. Now, stand up. I'll help you dry off." His grin turned lascivious. "And I want a good look at you."

For some reason, the heat in his eyes was her undoing. Tobias was a strong, rugged man. He could -- and likely did -- have any woman he wanted. Kitty knew she was a novelty to him, one he'd likely tire of quickly because she had no experience. At all.

She took his hand, and he pulled her to her feet. When she would have stepped out of the tub, Tobias simply wrapped his arms around her and lifted her out, setting her on her feet by the vanity. "Don't move," he said. He might have been grinning at her, but his eyes had gone very serious.

Kitty crossed her legs and covered her breasts with her arms, but, honestly, he'd already seen most of what she had to offer. What was this one thing?

"Wish you wouldn't cover up," he muttered as he took a towel and wrapped it around her. It was so large, it wrapped around her whole body twice. She felt like she was drowning in terry cloth, but it covered her. Guess she couldn't have it both ways.

"It's a little hard not to," she muttered. "You're a bit intimidating."

Tobias moved so that his hips were wedged between her legs. When she might have tried to keep them shut, he simply used his hands to shove them farther apart. Kitty thought about protesting, but he wasn't trying anything and if she were honest, she was way the fuck turned-on.

Once again, that tantalizing smell of Tobias surrounded her. Kitty could just close her eyes and inhale deeply until there was no way she'd ever forget that scent.

"You know I ain't gonna hurt you. Right?"

She nodded.

"Words, baby. I need to hear that you agree. If not, then I need to work a little harder earning your trust."

"I know you won't hurt me. You've had all kinds of opportunities to these last two weeks. Especially that first night when I was high on painkillers."

"Good. Now. I've let you live here for two weeks," he started. He used kind of a sing-song voice as he ticked off each thing he'd done for her. "Got you a job, got a doc to look at your knee and keep you high, and I've waited on you hand and foot so you'd be comfortable and could heal." His grin was boyish until he spoke again. Then it turned positively wolfish. "I think it's time you gave me something in return."

"If this is the part where you tell me I have to sleep with you, you can piss off," she grumbled, but there was a smile tugging at her own lips she knew Tobias didn't miss.

He put his hand over his heart. "You're wounding me, baby."

"Somehow I think you'll be fine."

"I wasn't going to demand you sleep with me. You'll do that on your own." He waited a moment before speaking. Probably expecting her to throw a barb at him. Truth was, her mouth went dry at the thought. He was right. She'd likely jump him before this was over. Especially if he kept up this full-court press with her. When she just stared at him, he continued. "I simply want a kiss. Is that too much to ask? Just one little kiss?"

Before she could form a response in her addled brain, Tobias leaned into her and pressed his lips to hers gently. It was nothing more than a soft touch of skin, but it felt like so much more. Kitty's world narrowed to the slight contact as he just brushed his mouth back and forth over hers. She whimpered, but kept her lips closed because, really, she'd never kissed anyone before. This was all new territory for her. And she was both terrified and titillated.

Tobias wasn't impatient with her, just continued his gentle seduction. When he grazed his tongue over her lips, Kitty couldn't stop the soft gasp that escaped her throat. He grunted before sweeping his tongue along the inside of her bottom lip slowly. On some level, she realized she could easily pull back if she wanted. But she didn't. Instead, she stayed very still, her lips parted, letting him lap as he wished.

There was no denying Tobias was an expert at both seduction and kissing. Kitty wanted to participate, but didn't know what to do. She'd never been so frustrated and utterly humiliated in her life. She couldn't hope to entice a man like Tobias. She didn't even know how to kiss, for crying out loud!

"Just relax, baby," he coaxed. "I'll do the work. You just do what feels good."

Oh, God! Did he realize she'd never kissed a man before? Who was she kidding? Of course, he knew! He was a biker. A member of a motorcycle club. Didn't they have women falling all over them? Probably fucked a different woman every night. How many women had he kissed compared to her single kiss? The thought made her whimper and shove at his chest. She loved what he was doing to her mouth with his tongue and teeth. Loved it so much she was squirming on the vanity surface. But she couldn't let him do more. If she did, she'd lose herself, and she'd never be able to look at him or any member of Salvation's Bane again. She had to work with these people. Or, at least, there'd be no way to avoid them if she took him up on his offer to work at the gym, which she'd already done.

"Stop," she whispered, barely holding on to her tears when she just wanted to curl up into a ball and sob like a baby.

"You don't want me to stop. You're as turned-on as I am."

"I still want you to stop." How she managed it

she'd never know. Pushing at his chest a little harder, Kitty slid to the floor gingerly, careful of her knee, and hurried out the door. Thankfully, there was a decent-sized closet with a light. She snagged a pair of underwear and hurried inside, shutting the door behind her. No doubt he'd come after her, but she intended to be dressed before he did. Thankfully, he gave her several seconds before he knocked on the door.

"Kitty? Come out."

"I'm dressing. Give me a minute."

"You're composing yourself. If I'm gonna be all fucked-up and horny, so are you. Get your luscious little ass out here." Tobias didn't sound angry. Hopefully, he wasn't. She needed this job. And his house. If he kicked her out now…

The thought spurred her to hurry, and she stepped out of the closet moments later. Thankfully, she'd managed to don a pair of gym shorts and a longish T-shirt before she did. As she knew would happen, Kitty couldn't quite meet his gaze when she stepped out, opting instead to focus on the floor a few feet to his right.

"You OK?"

"Fine," she said automatically.

Tobias sighed. "You're anything but fine. Look at me," he demanded. Immediately, she did, wishing to God she could refuse. There was just something about that particular tone of voice that had her jumping to obey him. "I'm not gonna hurt you, honey. I'm not gonna force myself on you, either. Not gonna lie and say I won't kiss you again. I intend to. But it doesn't go any further unless you want it to."

"I can't." Why she said that she had no idea. She should have kept her stupid mouth shut.

"Why not? Ain't no rule against it."

"It's just not a good idea."

He tilted his head at her, studying her too closely for her peace of mind. "You're a virgin." It wasn't a question.

Instantly, her face went beet red. "That's none of your business." Kitty tried to sound firm, but it came out a squeak.

"Nope," he agreed. "It ain't. It *is* important, though. Because, if I'm gonna be your first, I need to know it. Last thing I want to do is hurt you."

Her gaze snapped up to his. "Who says you're gonna be my first?"

He gave her that lopsided, cocky grin she found hard to resist. "Oh, I say, baby. I'm gonna definitely be your first."

"Look." It was best she try to inject some common sense into the situation before it got too far out of control. "Let's just lay this out there. Yes. I'm a virgin. Until a moment ago, I'd never even kissed a guy. Having said that, there's no way for you to think I could remotely satisfy you in bed. You'd have to teach me everything. I don't know the simplest things. I've never even watched a porno, for crying out loud!" As she spoke, Tobias's smile got wider and wider. His eyelids half closed, a look of complete satisfaction on his face. She stopped trying to make her point. "What?" she demanded instead.

"You're just making me more determined. Teachin' little innocents usually isn't my thing, but I'll make an exception for you." He crossed his arms over that massive, delectable chest she'd been idolizing for two weeks now. "How about this. I promise I'll make it good for you. I'll teach you anything you want to know. I'll let you explore my body to your heart's content. I'll even give you free access to do anything you want to do, anytime you want to do it. In return, you'll let me teach you anything *I* want, you'll let *me* explore *your* body to my heart's content, and you'll give me free access to do anything I want to do, anytime I want to do it."

Holy.

Fuck.

"Sounds… uh… No!" She shook her head firmly, but she swallowed nervously. Because she was intrigued beyond her wildest dreams. "That's a really bad idea."

"Is not. You're a brave girl. You have to be to do all that shit you do in the gym. Think of me as your partner. You let a complete stranger throw you up in the air before. I won't be letting you out of my arms. It's got to be safer."

"Yeah. I let a complete stranger toss me up in the air. Look what it got me! Better a broken kneecap than a broken…" She stopped herself before she could finish the sentence. "Nope. Not a good idea."

He chuckled. "We'll see. Come on. I'll take you to the gym. Today's your first lesson. From what I hear, the kids are lined up just waiting to see you. Seems you've already made a huge impression."

She had? Kitty couldn't help the smile. When she thought about the kids at the gym, her heart melted. Rabid gymnastics moms aside, she loved every single one of them. Some of the older ones could be catty, but they were mostly just typical teenagers. The younger ones were just precious.

"I can take an Uber."

"Over my dead body," he said, frowning for the first time. "It's not safe."

"Everyone takes them, and I don't have a car."

"Don't need a car." He spread his arms wide. "You've got me."

"Great," she muttered. "Just fucking great."

Chapter Six

"Hey, Tobias!" Stryker called out from across the gym. Glitter, his woman, was down on the floor with some of the younger kids doing a dance class. Kitty had jumped at the chance to combine dance and gymnastics. She and Glitter had hit it off immediately. Turned out, Glitter had a bit of a tumbling background as well as dance, so things were going great in that department. With her background in competitive gymnastics, Kitty had some dance background, but she loved Glitter's moves and was determined to incorporate them into some of the girls' routines. She said it was the one thing about competition she always felt was lacking. The "dancing" during the floor routine was always stiff and awkward. She wanted it to be exciting for the girls as well as pretty on the floor. So Kitty eagerly started incorporating Glitter's dancing with her tumbling.

"You stayin' to keep an eye on Glitter?"

"Someone has to. Besides, I need you to go find something for me. I'll stay here and watch over the girls."

"Oh? What'd you lose?"

Stryker waved him off. "Not me. You."

Tobias narrowed his eyes. "Not following."

"Well, you've claimed your woman but not in front of the club. You've not even been to the club since you brought her home. I figure she forbid you to go, so I'mma need you to find your man card. Check her panty drawer first."

Tobias took a swing at his brother. Stryker was clearly expecting it since he ducked neatly and backed away, laughing like a fucking hyena.

"Laugh it up, motherfucker. I remember how

you were with Glitter."

"Yeah, but no one else does that. You're in the spotlight now."

"Fucker."

"Seriously, I've got some information for you."

"From Justice?"

"Oh, yeah. Seems your boy Sanfried Hammer had something to do with Rycks getting fucked up a couple of weeks ago. Hammer's men took one hell of a beating. One of 'em got to be gator bait."

That surprised Tobias. "I knew the fucker had something going on, just not that it was close to us. He used Kitty to get into the gym, didn't he?"

"Not Kitty. Coach Shannon. Kitty was a convenient message after he got whatever it was he wanted. To Coach Shannon. Not us. From what Justice can dig up, he had no idea you were here. He does now. Bettin' he comes in full force if he comes back, and I'm sure he'll come back."

"Next time I see that fuckin' bastard, I'm killin' him. Don't care if it's the middle of downtown with the whole fuckin' state as witnesses. He's a fuckin' dead man."

"Just sit tight. You may not have to lift a finger. Justice says word is El Diablo himself is on this one."

Tobias grunted, nodding in satisfaction. "Guess he didn't take to kindly to anyone fuckin' with his people."

"Guess not. Apparently, Hammer's into some heavy stuff. He's pissin' off the wrong people in high places. Not sure if he's a mastermind or a dumb fuck. Either way, he's got the attention of more than one scary person. It's a toss-up as to who gets him first. Justice says they're bettin' heavily on El Diablo."

"Guess Justice didn't factor me into the

equation."

"Oh, he did. Which surprised me. Justice knows why you want Hammer taken out. Apparently, El Diablo has more."

"Thorn know about this?"

"Yeah. It's why I'm here. He told me to make you understand that under no circumstances are you to go after Hammer. If he turns back up in Palm Beach where we can get him, Thorn said he'd take care of him."

"So, basically, he just wants me to keep my nose clean because of our connection."

"Not basically. That's it exactly. Face it. When your sister was injured, you weren't exactly quiet about your disdain for the man. You kill him, the cops'll be all over you."

"It'd be worth it. The shit that man has done to my family…"

"Yeah. And you goin' to jail for killin' him would be worse."

"You guys'd take care of Sansa and Kitty. They'd be protected."

"Not the same as havin' you with them."

Tobias was silent for a while. "I will see that fucker dead, Stryker."

"I know. And I'll have your back. But we're gonna do it Thorn's way. We don't, and Cain will have our asses. Much as I respect the man, he tends to take up a place."

"We don't belong to Bones," Tobias said instantly. "They can't police us."

"No, but we also work for ExFil. Cain won't tolerate us going outside direct orders from our president. He'd consider it mutiny and would certainly fire you from ExFil. Might even convince Thorn to expel you from Bane, and before you disagree, think about it. This is Cain we're talkin' about. The man is all about control."

"He's also all about family, and Bane is family."

Stryker jumped on that. "Exactly! And if you put Bane in danger as a whole by not following orders, don't think he won't cull the herd."

He had a point. "Fine. But this fucker does not get to live."

"Pretty sure that's already being taken care of. If not by El Diablo, then by someone Thorn's designated. My guess would be Bohannon and Sword from Bones. We aren't involved, and no one can connect Bones to the crime."

"Blood will likely clean their trail and Data any digital footprints they might leave behind."

Stryker nodded in agreement. "So, yeah. They've got this. Trust Thorn like you always do."

"He's my brother, same as the rest of you. It's still hard to trust on something this big." He nodded to a couple of the guys training with Salvation's Bane at the gym. "Noticed several of them here today."

"Yeah. They're considering it part of their training. Keeping them on the lookout for anything suspicious."

"With so many kids here, not to mention my woman, it's a damned good idea."

"One, I'd like to point out, that was suggested by Thorn."

Tobias sighed. "Fine. I admit I can be an overprotective bastard who thinks he's better than anyone else at keeping the people he cares about safe. Satisfied, you bastard?"

"Oh, absolutely. I'll pass your thanks on to Thorn." He grinned. "In the meantime, go find that man card."

* * *

Kitty mopped a towel over her face. Sweat covered her body, and she felt wonderful. The kids had kept her on her toes, but she loved every second of it. Now that she was the one setting the training regimen, she was more enthusiastic about it. She'd never questioned Coach Shannon's motivations, but Kitty had thought from the first day she'd been there that the woman didn't even try with these kids unless they were on her personal roster.

The results were phenomenal. She'd found several treasures in the bunch, and several who were eager to push themselves but hadn't been given the opportunity. For the first time since she'd blown her knee out before the trials, she had a sense of purpose. And it wasn't just with gymnastics.

As if her thoughts had summoned him, she saw Tobias trot down the stairs from the observation balcony and offices above the gym floor.

"Hey, Kittycat!"

Uh-oh. He'd taken to calling her that over the last couple days. It was always a preamble to him kissing or touching her in a way that curled her toes.

"I'm busy, Tobias," she called, hoping he'd keep his distance and hoping he wouldn't at the same time. The gym was clearing out, but there were several men -- probably from the group Salvation's Bane was training -- scattered throughout the place. She'd noticed them when she and Tobias had opened the gym this morning but hadn't really given them much thought.

"Not that busy. You got somethin' I need." He stalked toward her, purpose in every step.

"Uh-oh," Glitter said as she finished up the last

of her class, sending the girls on their way. "He's got that look in his eyes."

"What look?" Kitty asked the question even as she knew the answer.

"The one that says you're about to get taken to bed. Fast."

Tobias reached for her the second he was close enough and pulled her into his arms. "Been needin' this all fuckin' day, Kittycat." His lips met hers in a fiery-hot kiss. Whistles and calls from the men in the room filled the gym. The few girls still there giggled. So did Glitter, the goof ball. She was always trying to get Kitty to make the first move on Tobias. Apparently he'd gotten tired of waiting.

Just like always, the second his lips touched hers, Kitty went to a place where only Tobias existed with her. Anyone else in the immediate vicinity was forgotten, and she entered an exciting world where pleasure was the only important thing.

He swept his tongue inside her mouth in a long, slow sweep. She moaned and sagged against him, letting him hold her and guide her as he wanted. This seemed to please him greatly if the rumble of pure masculine satisfaction was anything to go by.

"Mmmm," he purred. "That's my little Kittycat."

"Tobias," she whispered. "We can't do this here. Everyone's watching, and the kids haven't all left yet."

He pulled her closer, tucking her head under his chin. "Don't worry, babe. I'll always take care of you. You done here?"

"Yeah," she sighed. She was sweaty and probably stank, but he didn't seem to care. It felt too good to be in his arms to worry about it, though. If he didn't mind, she'd make do until she could get a shower.

"Then we're going home."

"Wait!" She pulled back. Or, rather, tried to. Tobias just squeezed her tighter. "I have to put the equipment away."

"Not tonight, sweetheart. The guys can do it. You have something more important to do."

"I do?"

"Oh, yeah. We're going home. Once we get there, you're about to be rid of that pesky virginity."

"What?" The word was more of a squeak.

"Yup. I'm done waiting for you to come to me. Was a stupid move on my part since you're likely intimidated by me."

"I -- I am not! You don't intimidate me! I'm not afraid of you, Tobias, and fuck you for saying I was!"

That got a laugh from him. Apparently, she'd played right into his hands. He'd wanted her back up, and she'd given him the reaction he was looking for. It just made her all the more furious at him.

"Come on, honey. We're going." Instead of taking her hand or guiding her by a hand on her back, Tobias scooped her up in his arms and carried her outside. All the way, the men around them laughed and called out to Tobias.

"Don't do anything I wouldn't do!"

"Is that even possible?"

"Kitty, you show him who's boss!"

Tobias carried her out to his bike. He set her beside it and handed her the helmet on the back. "Put it on the dome and get on the bike."

She hesitated, but, honestly, she couldn't be mad. She loved riding behind him. Nothing felt so free as rolling down the highway on that Harley. It always made her horny, though she'd never told Tobias. She was fairly certain he'd figured it out. Her suspicion was confirmed when he took the long way around to his house. The five-minute ride took twenty, and every second of it the rumble of the motor seemed to buzz between her legs like an intimate vibrator keeping her turned-on the longer they rode. By the time they pulled into the garage at his house, Kitty was nearly whimpering with need because she knew she'd never deny him what they both wanted.

Tobias shut the bike down and held her arm while she swung her leg over the side to stand next to him. He followed, scooping her up in his arms. "Ride make you horny?"

"Yes," she breathed, wrapping her arms around his neck and nuzzling her face against his shoulder. She trembled with need and nervous energy. This was it. She was really going to do this. Why? Because she wanted Tobias. She was probably just another notch in his bedpost, but she could live with that. There was no way Tobias didn't make her first time the best experience of her life.

"Good." He grinned down at her as he made his way into the house. "Bike did its job."

"You don't think you could have done the same job? I mean, this is my first time. I want someone who's better at it than me."

He scowled, then pulled her higher so he could bury his face in her neck and tickle her with his mouth and beard. "Was that sass?"

She squealed with laughter, wiggling in his arms. Somehow he got them to the bedroom and tossed her onto the bed, following her down only to bury his face in her neck once again.

"Stop it! Oh, God!" She howled with laughter, pushing at him. Somehow, his tickling morphed into something altogether different. Her pussy tingled and her clit throbbed. Kitty found herself moaning loudly and arching her neck to give him better access.

"Still want me to stop, Kittycat?"

"I take it back," she groaned. "Don't you dare stop!"

Tobias chuckled, fastening his mouth on her neck in a wide grip and sucking gently. "Greedy for my touch?"

"Will you promise not to hurt me?" Kitty felt stupid asking the question. It was her first time. It was supposed to hurt. Only, if she were honest with herself, she didn't really mean physical pain, though that was a concern.

To her surprise, Tobias kissed her once, then pulled back to look at her. He lowered his full weight on top of her, taking his time to settle between her legs in the cradle of her hips. It was a long time before he spoke, and Kitty thought she might have pissed him off. She was just about to apologize when he stroked her face gently before leaning down to kiss her once more.

"I can't promise it won't hurt, baby. But I promise to prepare you and distract you enough it won't be too bad. Once the pain's over, I swear I'll make you feel so good you won't remember the pain."

Then he kissed her again, nipping and licking at her lips until she opened eagerly to him. God, the man could kiss! How could he make her whole body tingle with just his tongue caressing hers? Kitty clung to Tobias, moving against him restlessly. The longer he kissed her, the better it felt and the more she wanted him. It wasn't long before she couldn't stop her own whimpers and moans.

The next thing she knew, Tobias's hand was on the bare skin at her waist sliding upward to cup her breast through her sports bra. In the back of her mind, Kitty knew she was a sweaty mess, but she couldn't wrap her mind around anything other than the sensations Tobias was building inside her with his simple touches.

Before Kitty realized what was happening, Tobias had whipped off her T-shirt and shoved her bra up over her breasts. She gasped when he took one nipple into his mouth, humming around it as if it were his favorite treat. She gasped, unable to wrap her head around the sensations flooding through her. If this was what it was like all the time, why had she never tried this? Then he moved to the other breast and she was unable to think.

Tobias played her body like a finely tuned instrument. Everywhere he touched, a moan or whimper escaped her. For such a hard-looking man he had the gentlest touch. She had the feeling, though, he could be rough. He'd been nothing but kind to her since that first interaction when she got the impression he wasn't sure what to make of her. And, shit, he was moving down her body now! Her belly button, back up to nuzzle and lick her ribcage only to forge back down to just above her mound.

Dimly, she knew she hadn't showered and had been sweating all day. Somehow, that made it all the more erotic. But what would he think?

"Don't," she denied softly, trying to make herself push him away. Instead, her fingers tunneled into his hair and she held him to her.

He chuckled. "Which is it, Kittycat? You're holding my head still."

"I don't know! God!"

"Just Tobias," he said. "When I've made you come, you can call me God."

"Quit making fun of me!"

"Not making fun, baby. Tell me what you object to." Just like that, he stopped his teasing and acknowledged her fear.

"I stink." Kitty couldn't make herself say it too loudly, but it had to be said.

"Just good clean sweat, baby. Sex is supposed to be sweaty. Besides, it's your scent. Ain't covered up by soaps or perfumes or any of that other shit women use. Just all you."

Before she could protest again, Tobias lowered his face between her legs and latched on.

Had a woman ever tasted this good? Had she ever responded to him with such abandon? Tobias wasn't what one could call a giving lover. He took what he wanted and let his partner do the same. She didn't get off, it was on her. Kitty, on the other hand, made him want to make her come just to see what she looked and sounded like. She was already so out of control she was crying out and thrashing beneath him, her hips bucking so hard he had to pin her with a forearm across her pelvis. Liquid honey flowed freely from her with every lash of his tongue. Her little clit throbbed under his lips. That little hole beckoned him to pierce it, to take her virginity and fill her with his cum when he did. She was fresh. New. And all fucking his.

Tobias found himself grunting with every drop of liquid he drank from her. Going down on a woman had never really been his thing, but it was important he do everything in his power to please Kitty. He wanted this time to be special for her. Hell, it was going to be special. For both of them. Kissing each hip bone once, Tobias crawled back up her body and reached for the nightstand. A part of him wanted to say fuck the condom and just fuck Kitty. But he couldn't. Not this time, much as he wanted to. Next time. He'd spell it out. Once he came in her, he had the sneaking suspicion he'd never let her go. Probably because he'd never fucked a woman without one. Never felt the fucking need. Now, it was like a mantra in his mind. He could see his cum dripping out of her after he'd fucked her into oblivion.

Shaking his head, he tore open the packet and slipped the little son of a bitch on his dick before he could change his mind. Giving his cock one final pump, he positioned himself at her entrance.

"Ready, Kittycat?"

"I --"

"Ready for me to fuck my little pussycat?"

"Tobias!"

"I need the words, Kitty. Do you want me inside you?"

"Yes! Oh, God, yes! Please!"

"Deep breath, baby. Eyes on me."

Deliberately, he forced her to look at him, to stay in the moment. He didn't want to cause her pain, but he wanted her to stop him if she changed her mind. This had to be a conscious decision on her part, or there was no way he could keep her if she tried to run.

"That's it. Feel me. Feel me enter you. Can you?"

"Yes," she whispered, her eyes wide and very much focused on his. "It's stretching me. Burns a little."

"Embrace it!" he hissed. "Take the pain with all that pleasure. Can you do that?"

His words were like flipping a switch. She arched her neck, closed her eyes and screamed. Her pussy clamped down around him, and Tobias had to bite the inside of his cheek to keep from coming right there. She milked him, squeezed his cock like a vise. Her body was so tight around him it was difficult to concentrate and not just fuck her hard and fast. Soon. But not yet.

"That's it, baby. Come hard."

"T -- Tobias!" Kitty clung to him, her fingers biting into his sides. The little bite of pain was all that kept him grounded. Otherwise, he'd have lost himself in her. In a few minutes he could. But not now. This was her time.

Several seconds passed, and her body relaxed. When it did, Tobias lowered himself fully so that her breasts were mashed against his chest. "There, baby. Feel better?"

The bemused look she gave him was completely satisfying. "I didn't know…"

"And that's why I'm here. Gonna show you how fuckin' good sex is. Then, when you're ready, I'm gonna show you how much better it can get."

She groaned, but slid her arms around his neck. "Not sure I'll survive that."

"You will, Kittycat. I'll always be here to save you."

Then, Tobias started to move inside her once again. A steady in and out, getting her used to him and the new sensations. He kept a close eye on her, paying attention to make sure there was no discomfort before he started moving again. Kitty just rolled with it. If she hurt, there was no way to see it. She was as into this as he was.

Kitty didn't seem to be a woman who built slowly after her first orgasm of the night. The second he started to increase the speed and strength of his fucking, she responded to him, moving her hips in time with his. Whimpers and little sharp cries of passion filled the air as she clung to him, trying to keep up and damned near unmanning him. It took every ounce of discipline Tobias had to keep from coming. There was no way that was happening until she'd had all she could handle tonight.

Tobias was amazed at the strength in her tiny body. There was well-honed, fine muscle playing underneath her skin. Maybe that was why she showed no discomfort with her first time. She was as hardened as any warrior Tobias had ever met. Any pain she experienced, Kitty had likely had worse in the course of her life. To reach the level she had in her sport, she'd likely been training since she was a young child. She'd experienced pain in many forms all her life. If ever there was a woman who could take everything he was, everything he needed in sex, it was Kitty. If he introduced her to rough, hard sex with kindness and… and love, she would be his match in every way.

Tobias kissed her because he had to. Love never factored into sex for him. It was a biological function that gave pleasure and helped him fucking sleep. This… was not. This was something more. Something deep. He barely knew Kitty, but he knew she was made for him.

Kitty arched into him, digging her heels into his ass and her nails into his back. When he refused to move faster, she hissed, nipping his bottom lip and pulling him to her with her legs. Her nails scratched roughly down his flesh, probably leaving shallow furrows.

"My little kitten has fangs and claws," he growled.

"More." The soft sigh was a sharp contrast to her demanding actions. It seemed to suit Kitty. She was so gentle and patient with the kids she taught when

Tobias knew she demanded perfection of herself. He'd seen it as she worked out, doing handstand pushups, working her upper body instead of her legs. Blade had told her to stay off her knee, and she'd done it. But she hadn't missed a single workout. Just thinking about watching her move got him harder. She was poetry in motion. Now was no exception. He pulled back to watch her move. Her stomach rippled with sleek muscle as did her arms and shoulders. She was perfection.

Just when the imagery and his own thoughts were about to get the better of him, Kitty cried out, tightening her grip on him. Her little pussy clamped down on his cock and contracted. She screamed, the tendons in her neck standing out as the sound went on for several seconds. Tobias gave himself the go-ahead and plunged into her faster and faster. His thrusts were almost brutal as he rode her until his own orgasm slammed into him. He shouted, roaring to the ceiling before collapsing on top of Kitty, still thrusting as if needing to get every single drop of his cum inside her. Damn the fucking condom.

"You OK, baby?" He was panting, still trying to get his breath.

"Yeah." Her sigh was sweet and soft. "Better than OK."

Tobias found her mouth and kissed her, lapping at her lips and tongue. They did that for long, long moments. Tobias could happily have gone again, but he didn't want to make her sore.

Taking care, he rolled off her enough to pull out, sliding off the condom and knotting it. The trash can was beside the bed, thankfully, and he dropped the condom inside it. Then he pulled the covers over them, pulling Kitty snugly against him.

"Rest for a bit. Then we'll take a shower."

"Mm-hmm," she agreed sleepily, her eyes already closed. Tobias tucked her head underneath his chin and just dozed with her. It was the first time in his life he'd ever actually slept with a woman.

And here he'd thought she was the virgin.

Chapter Seven

"We're having church at the gym. Clear a room." Normally, Thorn would never have suggested having a club meeting outside of the clubhouse, but this was a special circumstance. Tobias was only too happy to comply.

"Already done. Got news on that bastard, Hammer?"

"I'll explain it all when we meet. Keep those trainees and the prospects on guard. If we keep letting the community use the gym, we're going to have to maintain security until the situation is resolved."

This sounded serious. Tobias knew better than to discuss club business on the phone, though. Even though Ripper had made sure everything was secure with all the phones owned by the members or in buildings owned by Salvation's Bane, there was still that small chance someone could monitor their communications. Not likely, but it was always wise to play it safe.

"Understood. We'll be ready."

Tobias watched Kitty with the girls in the gym from his loft above the floor. She had blossomed since she'd taken over the place. The only thing that marred her growth was his paranoia about Sanfried Hammer. That man was still out there. Watching the gym. Tobias knew it as sure as he knew his own name. The only question was what exactly the other man wanted. He had a feeling Thorn knew what was going on, and Tobias was pretty sure he wasn't going to like what Thorn was going to tell them during the meeting.

He took out his phone and called Lock. "You keep an eye on her. Kitty is your only responsibility. Anyone tries to tell you different, you tell them to come see me."

Lock grunted. His version of a "yes, sir."

He'd decided the meeting would take place in his office. Not only could he still keep an eye on Kitty, but he'd closed off the observation galley and had the parents segregated to a corner on the floor. He'd found, however, most of them simply dropped their kids off for the afternoon. That was something he was going to have to discuss with Kitty. If it was going to continue, he needed to make provisions for food. While some of the kids had well-off, if cheap, parents, some of the parents used this time to work and not have to worry about their child. It was something he needed to consider.

One by one, the Salvation's Bane patched members filed into his office. Thankfully, he'd built it with this very thing in mind. The guys often helped him with training outside groups, and this was the perfect place for meetings.

The second Thorn and Ripper, with Rycks from Black Reign, looking a little worse for wear, walked through the door, Tobias knew there was trouble. "Fuck," he muttered.

"Good way to describe it," Thorn said as he took a seat behind Tobias's desk as if he owned the joint. He smirked at Tobias as if he knew what the other man was thinking, and Tobias flipped him off. He had a feeling that was the last lighthearted exchange they'd all have for a while.

"What's goin' on?" Red, the club's mechanic and the biggest, scariest-looking son of a bitch Tobias had ever seen, crossed his arms over his chest and leaned a hip against the far wall next to the big one-way window overlooking the gym floor.

"Not only did Ripper and Justice find out what

was going on with Tobias's man, Hammer, but I've called El Diablo to help with this one."

A chorus of angry mutters all around followed.

"You can't be fuckin' serious."

"That son of a bitch? What the fuck, Thorn?"

"Fuck 'em all. We can take 'em by our fuckin' selves!"

Thorn didn't raise his voice. Rather he let the men carry on for a moment before raising his hand for silence. "Believe me, I don't like it any better than you, but this is a special circumstance. Lots of fuckers are gonna have to die. And I mean that literally." When the room quieted down, Rycks stepped forward.

"The man you know as Jackson Heart or Sanfried Hammer has many aliases. He's usually very careful about where he targets, but this gym and the arrangement it has as a community gym was just too good for him to pass up. It was just pure bad luck on his part he chose this place. If Tobias had his name attached to the gym and not Salvation's Bane, the bastard would have known he needed to pick another target, no matter how tempting this one was. He had no idea he was choosing a victim in a place protected by a relation of one of his other victims. Even then, I'm not certain he'd have done the smart thing and left your place alone."

"Wait," Tobias interrupted. "Are you saying there is a possibility he'd have risked coming here even knowing he would have run into me? Because that sounds an awful lot like you're suggesting he's suicidal." He was only half joking. Suicidal or not, no way that son of a bitch lived past the exact day Thorn gave the go ahead to kill him.

"He's not suicidal. He's just evil in the worst possible way."

"Pedophile?"

"Yes, but that's not even the biggest issue." Rycks looked tired. Broken. It was a new look for the normally cocky bastard, and Tobias found himself not enjoying himself as he should have. "Sanfried Hammer is a sadist, but in the most twisted sense of the word. He likes to hurt people. Particularly people who trust him completely. Most especially children or teenagers and young adults."

The room fell silent.

"Why do I have the feeling you're oversimplifying things?" Tobias was getting a sick feeling in his stomach. He had to concentrate to keep it from escalating into a full-blown puke session.

"I don't fully understand it myself," Rycks continued, "but his M.O. seems to be to pick young women to work in his troupe of cirque performers. He and a few others in the group work with them daily. They earn their complete trust and confidence, then…"

"They help them have an accident," Tobias finished. "Let them get hurt intentionally."

"All while avoiding blame. At most, they'd be blamed for a bad throw. Anyone can slip, and the girls know the danger they're taking on when they volunteer."

"Volunteer isn't even close to the right word," Tobias muttered. "Most of those girls literally beg to work with him."

"Exactly," Rycks affirmed. "It's the ultimate high for him. He gets them doing ever more dangerous tricks, then watches them take the fall. He's not actually injuring them, but he might as well be. When you called him out after your sister had her accident, it was the first time anyone suggested he threw the trick on purpose."

"He did the same with Kitty."

"And had she not instinctively known how to land she'd likely have been hurt far worse than she was."

"Kitty didn't say anything about knowing how to land. I got the impression she was concentrating so much on the complicated routine it caught her completely off guard."

"I'm sure it did," Rycks said. "But she was an elite-level gymnast. She didn't get there without learning air awareness. Her body did the best it could to land her on her feet. Your sister wasn't so lucky."

"Or good." It all clicked into place for Tobias. "It was Kitty's experience and skill level that saved her. Not any conscious effort."

"Right." Thorn snagged Tobias's attention when he was about to let it drift back out the window to focus on Kitty. "Sansa was good, but not at the level Kitty is."

"Sansa never stood a chance against that bastard." Tobias saw the truth of it. "So, what's his goal? Obviously he has a plan or he'd have moved on when he realized I was ready to kill him to death." That got a chuckle from a couple of the younger members of Bane, but not much.

"The girls," Rycks said. "There is a concentration of underprivileged girls here he could coax into 'trying out' for Cirque America with the promise of wealth and fame. He's a master salesman. He wants to give his pitch to as many of these girls and their parents as he can. If he can get a flood of fresh bodies in, I think he's reached a point where he's ready to do more and more dangerous tricks until someone dies."

"You think he'll go so far as to kill someone outright?"

"No," was Rycks's immediate denial. "He's too smart for that. Make no mistake, he wants someone to die. He just isn't willing to get caught. If he does, he wants there to be plausible deniability. It's why he keeps changing his name. That, and he doesn't want his troupe to get the reputation of girls getting hurt. Every few years he changes it and migrates his brand. He has three core members who stay with him because he gives them their addiction. Occasionally one gets out of line and he kicks them out for a while, but he never severs ties with them. Probably how he keeps them from ratting him out."

"So, he's trolling." Thorn stroked his beard as he thought about it. "I agreed to let El Diablo handle this, but in exchange, I want to know why. You seem a little more vested in this than I'd like. Last thing I want is you going off and getting yourself killed and raising questions as to what the fuck happened."

Rycks didn't even flinch. "I've got this under control. Nothing will come back to you. If all goes well, no one will ever realize the group did anything other than leave town without the girls they promised to take with them."

"Yeah," Stryker spoke up for the first time. He'd been sitting quietly in the corner during the conversation. "Like you did when they beat the fuck outta ya."

"I didn't realize what I was dealing with. I thought it was only one guy. He got away pretty much unscathed. The other three didn't."

"I'm still havin' one of ours go with you. Tool and Trench from Bones are on their way here." Thorn sat back, his palms flat on the desk.

When Tobias opened his mouth to tell them all he was going to be involved, too, he was cut off. "You can't," Rycks denied instantly. "Especially not you, Tobias. You don't want the shit I'm gonna do coming back on you. Any of you."

"Which is exactly why they are coming with your crew." Thorn paused for a moment. "You *do* have a crew this time. Right?"

"Not above admitting I made a mistake. Or in thanking Salvation's Bane for getting me out of a tight spot." He gave a nod to the whole group. "Yes. I have a team this time. I don't make the same mistake twice."

"Then you won't mind if we tag along." Thorn's smile didn't in any way reach his eyes. Turning to Tobias, he added, "But not you. I want you as far away as possible when this goes down. In fact, you might think about takin' a trip."

Rycks had to have known this was coming because he simply shrugged. "Just tell them not to get in the fuckin' way. I don't want to accidentally maim them for life. Neither of 'em got women, do they? I won't take a man who's got a woman to protect."

That surprised Tobias, though he kept quiet. It was Thorn who answered. "No. I wouldn't send an attached man on an operation like this with a man outside our club."

Rycks barked a laugh. "I'll say one thing for you. I never have to question where I stand with you. Probably why El Diablo thinks so highly of you." Again, the statement surprised Tobias. Interesting.

"Good. Then we all know the expectations. You need to report to Blade. Won't let you go with my men if you're not a hundred percent."

"Anyone ever tell you you're a pushy bastard?"

Havoc snorted, giving Thorn a smug grin. The vice president been quiet until now, but even he couldn't resist that set up. "All the fuckin' time."

After the meeting, Tobias texted Lock to make sure he had an eye on the kids until they left, then made a beeline to Kitty. Without a word, he scooped her up and called over his shoulder, "Class dismissed."

Kitty called to her students. "Don't forget to stretch!" A chorus of giggles followed them down out of the room.

Tobias took her back to his office. The few remaining brothers took one look at his face, smirked, then made a hasty exit.

"Would you put me down?" Kitty sounded snippy, but he knew she'd be fine. Once he started playing with her. "What are you doing?"

"If it ain't obvious, then I'm doin' something wrong," he said, setting her on her feet. When he started undressing her, she sighed and helped him. "Really, Tobias. You need to let me get cleaned up at least one time before you jump on me. You might like the sex better if you did it when I was clean."

"Not possible to like the sex better. You're fuckin' *perfect*."

She started, like he'd thrown her, then grinned. "For a man everyone thinks is such a hard-ass, you say the nicest things."

"Besides, ain't gonna fuck you all sweaty this time." He picked her up and headed to the bathroom inside his office. Thank God he kept it clean and, more importantly, it had a shower. The stall was small, but both of them could fit inside it since she was such a little thing.

"What are you doing?"

"You wanted a shower, didn't you?"

"Well, yeah. Just didn't expect you to let me have one." She sounded amused, surprised, and maybe even a little disappointed.

"Kittycat, I'll give you anything you fuckin' want." He adjusted the water, then stripped his own clothes off.

"Uh, Tobias?" Kitty's gaze was glued to his tattooed, muscled torso. "What are you doing?" Tobias couldn't help but grin.

"What's it look like I'm doin'?"

"I thought you said I was gonna shower?" She still looked like she was mesmerized. She even took a step forward and ran her hand down his chest and abdomen lovingly. The touch made his cock hard as a fucking pole.

"You are. I'm showerin' with you."

That seemed to break her out of her trance. She looked up at him, an annoyed look in her eyes. "Now, why didn't you suggest that before? We've been doing this a solid month now! What the hell, Tobias?"

He barked out a laugh. "Why didn't *you* suggest it?"

Kitty crossed her arms over her chest, equal parts irritation and embarrassment on her face. "'Cause I never thought of it."

"Well, that's what you have me for. Besides, this is the first time I've been able to wait that long."

Tobias scooped her up and stepped into the tiny shower. She giggled. "Well, technically, you're probably not waiting as long because you always take me home before we have sex. Now, we're showering in your office and I'm pretty sure you ain't waitin' until we get home for sex."

"We definitely ain't waitin' until we get home." For some reason, the fact that she referred to his place as "home" filled him with satisfaction. Even though he'd never thought he'd ever keep a woman of his own -- penance for not protecting his sister -- the thought of her leaving him made him want to punch something.

He let her slide down his body under the wet spray. Those wide, innocent eyes of hers called to him on a purely primitive level. The second her feet were on the floor, he pulled out the pins in her braid. He had no intention of washing her hair, but he wanted to tug it at his leisure. Nothing in his life had prepared him for the way Kitty had taken over his life, his thoughts, his very soul. Now, knowing they were getting ready to hunt the man who'd hurt her and he was sidelined was killing him. It was for the best, but he didn't have to like it.

Taking the shower gel from the little built-in shelf, he squirted a dollop into his palm, then proceeded to scrub every inch of her skin with his hands. He paid special attention to her breasts and pussy, loving the feel of her bare mound and stiff nipples. Kitty leaned into him, letting him explore her body as he liked. She spread her legs so he could pet her easily and nearly purred as he stroked her from behind. Her little clit was hard and her pussy wet. On impulse, Tobias pressed his finger deeper as he trailed it from her opening to her ass.

She stiffened in his arms, but didn't pull back. "Tobias?" The look she gave him said she needed reassurance. Of course it was the first time she'd been touched back there. It was entirely possible she'd never even touched herself there beyond cleaning.

"Um?" He grinned at her, raising an eyebrow. When she didn't protest, he continued stroking her. The pad of his finger circled her little anus, pressing slightly every now and then. She squirmed in his arms, moving her body to slide over his. When he didn't do anything more than move his finger over her, teasing her, she let out a strangled cry.

"Oh, God, just do it already!"

"Do what, little Kittycat?"

She glared at him. "You know what!"

"Fine," he said, grinning as he bent down and took her mouth. She opened for him, tightening her arms around his neck and kissing him for all she was worth. Tobias still rubbed her ass, not penetrating her but teasing her with what could be. She started thrusting her hips back at him, trying to get his finger inside her, but he always backed off.

Finally, she bit his lip sharply. It hurt, but he still laughed, holding her close to him. "Woah, there, Kittycat. Don't bite so hard."

"Why should I do what you want when you won't do what I want?" Her face was flushed, and her breathing came in little pants.

"Honey, all you have to do is tell me what you want. I can't read minds."

"You know! Why are you trying to make me say it?" She nearly screeched at him.

"I can't read minds, Kittycat. You want something you gotta tell me. Besides…" He winked at her. "I want to hear you talkin' dirty to me."

She groaned and thumped her head on his wet chest. While she was there, she must have gotten distracted, because she moaned, then licked his chest over to his nipple and took the little bud into her mouth. Tobias sucked in a sharp breath, nearly giving in to the impulse to impale her on his finger. He managed to resist. Just.

"Tobias," she said, looking up at him, her tongue still lapping gently at his nipple. "Will you finger-fuck my ass? I need it so bad."

Yeah. He was in so much trouble. He'd had plenty of women ask for lots and lots of dirty things.

For some reason, having Kitty look up at him, all innocence and goodness, made him want to come all over the fucking place.

With a groan, Tobias did as she asked, easily sliding one finger into her ass all the way. Kitty cried out, thrusting back to his hand as if it were the one thing she wanted most in the world.

"You gonna let me fuck you there, baby?"

"You can do anything to me you want. Just make it feel this good, and you can fuck me to hell and back."

"Might take you up on that. Definitely gonna fuck this ass. Come in it. Fucking make you *love* it."

"Oh, God!" She let her head fall back and Tobias took advantage, latching on to her neck. He sucked, loving it as the sounds she made vibrated over his lips. "Oh, God, Tobias! I need you!"

"Tell me what you need, Kittycat. Be as dirty as you need to be."

She replied without hesitation in a husky, desperate voice. "I need you to fuck me. Put your cock in my pussy so I can ride you till I come." She hooked a leg around his hip, pulling herself up so that his cock rubbed over her bare mound.

"Motherfuck," he hissed at her neck. Had anything ever felt so good? Her pussy lips surrounded his cock, soaking him with her dewy heat. The water from the shower danced over his skin like warm summer rain, and the woman in his arms clung to him so sweetly he never wanted to let her go. It was more than sex. More than pleasure for either of them. To Tobias, this was a measure of what he wanted in his life from here moving forward. He wanted the love of this woman. He wanted her body, mind, and heart. He wanted everything he did in life to be with her in mind. Her happiness and wellbeing.

All these things ran through his mind like a fleeting dream that lingered just out of reach. He wanted it all. Wanted Kitty for his own. In his home.

In his heart.

With a frustrated growl, he fisted his hand in her hair and pulled her head back and took her kisses. She gave them willingly, lapping at his tongue like her delicate little kitty cat namesake. Didn't she realize how close he was to taking what he wanted and taking over her life? Tobias knew he could take her right now in the shower and she'd probably accept that he'd done so without discussing not using a condom and without her consent to do so. She'd look to him for guidance because, until he'd taken her virginity, she'd truly been an innocent. Still was in many ways. It would be the single worst thing he'd ever done in his life bar none if he did. Yet he was considering it even as he knew he'd burn in hell. The only thing that stopped him was the knowledge that Kitty would hate him forever when she'd realized what he'd done.

Then she had to go and ruin his good intentions by grinding over his cock while she tongue-fucked him.

"Tobias," she whispered. "You feel so good. Your cock rubbing my clit…"

"Little fucking witch," he hissed. "I'm not fuckin' you here. I'm not!"

"But I need you so much." She sounded like she was in pain, real tears in her voice. "You've made me crave you. You're like a drug. I can't get enough!"

"Baby, I -- FUUUUUCK!"

Kitty slid over his cock one last time before tilting her hips so the tip of his cock made contact with her entrance. Instead of backing off, however, Kitty sank down on him until he entered her, breaching that little pussy with a slow, steady glide until he was in as far as he could go.

"Goddammit, Kitty! I'm trying to be good here!"

"Don't want you good." She licked at his lips, then nipped the bottom one sharply before moving to take his earlobe between her teeth. "I need you *bad…*"

Then she started to move on him. Up and down, her strong thighs circling his hips and digging into his ass. That wet heat inside her surrounded Tobias, making a mockery of all his good intentions. She'd locked her ankles at the small of his back and didn't seem to be in any hurry to let him go. Her little whimpers and moans filled the small space, caressing him like another set of hands along his skin. Faster and faster she went, humming and moaning and whimpering with every move. Her cries grew louder until she finally threw her head back and screamed, her cunt milking him for all he was worth. And that was when all his good intentions went out the door.

With a desperate plea, Tobias tried to push her off him. "You've got to let me go, baby." Was his voice shaking? "Gonna come, and I can't come inside you."

"Please," she whimpered, her face next to his ear. Her arms and legs tightened around him even as she continued to rock her hips. "I want to feel your cum inside me. I want to know what it's like, and I want it to be you, Tobias. No one else. Only you."

Those were the magic words. His cock and balls didn't need any more encouragement. With a brutal yell and several hard thrusts, Tobias gave Kitty exactly what she'd asked for. He filled her with his cum. Clinging to her, he stayed as far inside her as he could, wrapping his arms so tightly around her he was afraid she couldn't breathe.

When it was over, when his mind and body were once again his own, he sighed. Pulling back to look at her he shook his head. "What am I going to do with you?"

She shrugged, looking slightly ashamed. "Keep me?"

Everything in Tobias stilled. *She'd done this on purpose.* But why? Sure, he was her first lover. Everyone was possessive over their first if it was a positive experience, but this was a bit extreme.

"Looks like we have some things to discuss," he said gently as he pushed a damp curl that had escaped her braid away from her face.

She ducked her head. "Are you mad at me?"

"Baby, I got what I wanted. No way I'm going to be mad at you over that. I do wonder why you did it. This could have some life-altering repercussions."

"You mean me getting pregnant? Yeah. I thought of that."

"And?"

She shrugged, her face heating to a lovely shade of pink.

Tobias sighed and shut off the water. Stepping out, he didn't separate their bodies, instead choosing to stay inside her as long as he could. He set her on the vanity of the small sink and framed her face with his hands, forcing her to look into his eyes.

"I'm not going to lie to you, Kitty. I'm not a good man. I have a dark and dangerous past and a lot of demons that revolve around Sanfried Hammer. Jackson Heart. Whatever his name is." He kissed her gently before he continued. "I intend on seeing that son of a bitch dead."

"I'm not asking you for anything, Tobias," she interrupted before he could finish. "But, I won't lie either. I was *hoping* that, if you did get me pregnant, you'd let me stay with you?" God, she was breaking his heart.

He sighed. "Baby, you know it doesn't work like that. Having a baby doesn't make a relationship." He winced when she looked like he'd struck her. She ducked her head again but not before he saw the sheen of tears in her eyes. "Look at me, Kitty." When she shook her head, he gently pinched her chin between his fingers and forced her to comply. As he suspected, tears overflowed and ran down her cheeks. "I'm not trying to be mean, or to let you down gently. I just wanted you to think about what you did. How it could backfire on you. Do you understand?"

She nodded. "I do, but…" Her gaze slid away from him, but he cupped her face once more and brought her focus back on him.

"But what?"

"But, I figured you were so protective, you'd do anything you could to keep a child of yours safe. Even if that meant taking me in and keeping me safe too."

"Christ," he muttered, pulling her in for a tight hug. He held her like that for a long time. The only reason he let her go was that she'd started shivering slightly. The stupid air conditioner vent was directly above them. Even with their shared body heat, it was getting chilly. He pulled a towel down from the cabinet next to the sink and wrapped it around her shoulders.

"Kitty, I will always keep you safe. As long as you need it. Also, at the risk of rewarding your bad behavior --" He gave her a stern look he didn't really feel. "-- I have no intention of letting you leave me for any reason. Baby or not. I'm making you mine at the first available opportunity."

She gasped, her eyes going wide and round.

"Really?"

"Don't congratulate yourself yet, girl. I ain't easy to live with."

"You're not?" She looked confused. "So… what's going to be different from the last month?"

He sighed. Had him there. "You're going to be a handful." His still semi-hard cock slid free of her, and he groaned softly. "Fuuuuck."

She giggled. It was the most beguiling sound he'd ever heard. "I'm sorry I tricked you," she said. Tobias didn't think she really meant it.

"Yeah, well, you may regret it one day. Won't matter, though."

"You promise?"

He kissed her softly once again. "Yeah, Kittycat. I promise."

Chapter Eight

The deal was, Tobias and Kitty were supposed to be on a fucking beach somewhere soaking up the sun. Far away from the carnage getting ready to take place. Instead, Tobias had left her in the care of Glitter, Alizay and Fleur. The women had been only too happy to spend time with his woman. All from the safety of the clubhouse. Surrounded by the entirety of Salvation's Bane. Yeah. He'd locked her down tight for this. If Thorn knew, he'd kick his ass, but he figured what his president didn't know wouldn't hurt either of them.

"You know Thorn's gonna kick your ass. Right?" Lock crept close behind him, nearly scaring the shit out of him, but Tobias managed to keep control of himself, never even flinching.

"Only if he finds out."

"Oh, he'll find out. If nothing else, Rycks will rat you out." That was Stunner. Did everyone know he'd snuck out when he was supposed to be with Kitty?

"Only if he wants his ass kicked." Even as he spoke, Tobias never took his gaze from his target.

"Already had that." Rycks's voice was quiet and on his other side. Thankfully, Tobias heard him approach not too long after Lock and wasn't as startled. *Oorah*, Marine Corps. "Don't want a repeat."

Not paying attention to the two men, he noticed Hammer and four other men moving about the apartment Tobias and the others were watching. The five of them appeared to be arguing fiercely. Tobias recognized one of the men as the one who'd been with Hammer at the gym. "Then you'll keep this under your hat."

"He might," Thorn's voice came behind them all. That made Tobias turn away from his target. *Shit*. "Still ain't nothin' happenin' in my fuckin' club I don't know about."

Tobias sighed. "It was the girls. Wasn't it?"

"You wanted to keep this a secret, find your own damned babysitter. The second you were out of the room, Alizay called Lucy for a 'girl's night in,' and my wife took off without me."

Tobias shrugged, turning back to the apartment. The men were still arguing, and it appeared to be escalating. "Not like she went far. You two spend more time at the clubhouse than your own home."

"That's changin'. Got a room to get ready for the baby, and I don't like makin' love to my ol' lady where any of you horny motherfuckers can hear."

Soft chuckles.

"Somethin's happenin'," Lock said. "Rycks. Take a look."

As they watched, Tyger Wilson, the man who'd accompanied Hammer to the gym, became animated, obviously upset. The other men were just as vehement in making their case. The only one who seemed unaffected was Hammer himself. He stood behind the other men, his arms crossed over his chest as if letting the others fight his battle for him.

"Any minute now…" Rycks studied the men through binoculars, just like Tobias and Rycks. The men from Salvation's Bane swapped out glasses from time to time, but Rycks just watched on impassively. Finally, Rycks muttered, "Heard enough, Shotgun. Take 'em."

Even before the words were out of his mouth, Tyger Wilson pulled a suppressed .45 and shot all four men in rapid succession. Head shots.

"Son of a bitch," Tobias gasped.

"What the fuck, Rycks?" Thorn's voice was soft,

but he sounded as angry as Tobias had ever heard him. "You planned an op *around* us?"

"Good job, Shotgun. Call in Fury and Samson. Clean the place, then get the fuck out." Rycks turned his attention from the men in the apartment, but didn't put down his field glasses. "I told you I had it covered. You're the one who insisted on sending your people in."

"Fucker," Thorn muttered. "You tell El Diablo I don't appreciate this, and I will damned well kick his ass if I ever see him again."

Rycks put the field glasses back to his eyes, covering his people until the job was done. "Oh, you'll see him again. Tell him yourself."

Thorn swore again before addressing Tobias. "You and Stunner get the fuck back to the clubhouse. Anything goes south I don't want you anywhere near this. Lock and I will stay here with our friend from Black Reign and make sure everything's taken care of."

"Fucker," Rycks muttered.

"Same." Thorn's growl would have sent a lesser man running. Rycks just flipped him off without taking the binoculars from his eyes.

"Well, that was rather anticlimactic." Stunner scrubbed his hand through his hair several times, probably unwilling to go until Tobias headed out. The fucker was like that. Always had his back, no matter what.

"This was my fight, Rycks." Tobias had wanted to be the one to kill that motherfucker. Wanted it with everything in him.

"Because of your sister? Or Kitty?" Rycks was a bastard. Tobias would tell him, too, if it weren't afraid he'd lose his shit.

"None of your fuckin' businiss," he snapped.

"Because either would be cause enough. End is still the same. Motherfucker's dead." Finally, Rycks looked up. "Go home to your woman and hold on to her instead of your hate. You can both help your sister heal."

Much as he hated to admit it, Rycks made sense. Tobias didn't have to like it, though.

* * *

The second Tobias opened the door, Kitty was off the couch and running into his arms. She jumped up and wrapped her arms and legs around him. No matter what he said, she still held a lingering fear he'd abandon her.

"Hey, baby," he said, hugging her tightly. "Everything's good."

"You didn't get hurt, did you?"

"No. I never even got close to the action. Fuckin' Rycks did him in before I had a chance to."

She sighed, rubbing her face against his. "Remind me to thank him."

"I will not. He took away my revenge."

"Just as well," she said. "I didn't want you going in the first place. Had I known you'd planned on killing him, I'd have protested harder."

"Baby, what did you think I was gonna do?"

"I don't know. Talk to him?"

"Right." He was amazed at how innocent Kitty could be. He loved that about her.

They stayed in the clubhouse that night, making love in his room more than once. Kitty tried to be quiet, but there just was no way to manage it. Tobias saw to that. Seemed he wasn't satisfied unless she screamed.

As they lay in the bed, clinging to each other and breathing heavily, Kitty was struck at how truly blessed she was.

"You promise you're not going anywhere?"

"Baby, wild dogs couldn't drag me away from you."

She relaxed a bit, a slow lethargy blanketing her every second she lay there in his arms. "Good. Because I'm pretty sure I love you."

He caught her under the chin and tilted her head up for a kiss. "I'm pretty sure I love you, too, Kittycat."

As the night moved on, and sleep claimed Kitty, she reflected on all that had happened since she'd come to Florida.

Had she known what awaited her, she might not have made the trek. If that had happened, she'd have missed out on so much in her life. She had no idea what the future held, but she knew she wanted it to include Tobias. Then it hit her.

"Tobias?"

"Umm?"

"You know, I don't even know your full name."

He stiffened beneath her before stroking her arm, apparently trying to cover the tension suddenly running through is body.

"Yeah? That important?"

She sat up, bracing herself on one arm. "Of course, it's important. How can I spend my life with you if I don't even know your name?" Then a thought struck her. "I -- I thought when you said you wanted me, you meant like the others want their women."

"You mean, as my ol' lady?"

"Well, yeah."

He cupped her cheek, pulling her back to him. "I do, Kittycat. I just want you to make sure it's what you want. We've got all the time in the world. Once I claim you, though, that's it. It's pretty much too late as it is. Everyone already knows where we're headed."

"Oh. Well. I still need to know your name."

"I need to know yours, too." He grinned at her. Which kind of irritated her. Which he likely intended.

"It's Katherine Delano."

"Hmmm… Like Roosevelt?"

"Yeah. I think my family was very, very distantly related to some branch of FDR's family tree. Like maybe even a bastard branch or something. But hey. You get what you get."

"Right."

When he didn't say anything further, Kitty prompted him. "So… your name?"

He was silent for so long, she thought he might not say anything. "It's McGuire. Tobias McGuire."

"Really? No biker name?"

He shrugged. "Tobias is cool enough."

She thought for a minute. Was about to doze off when it hit her. "Wait. McGuire. You mean, like Toby McGuire?"

"Toby is not my name, girl." He practically snarled the response.

Instead of being intimidated or hurt, she giggled. "Toby McGuire."

"Katherine…"

She giggled again.

"OK. That's it." He rolled them over and tickled her until she was squealing uncontrollably. "Laugh at me, will ya? Little witch!"

"Stop! Stop!" Kitty laughed and laughed until Tobias finally stopped, taking her mouth in a lingering, wet kiss. "I take it back," she said in a breathy voice. "Don't ever stop."

With a grin, Tobias deepened the kiss. "Never, baby. I'll never stop loving you."

Then Tobias proceeded to love Kitty the rest of

the night, well into the dawn hours. Kitty knew she'd be tired and maybe even a little sore as the day wore on. But it would be worth it. *Sooo* worth it.

Justice (Salvation's Bane MC 8)
Marteeka Karland

Justice: I expected to spend most of the rest of my life in prison. Even so, I worked for my club, Salvation's Bane, gathering valuable information about Palm Beach and all the clubs residing there. Imagine my surprise when a short, clumsy, curvy female comes to my rescue. The moment I see her in that prim skirt stretched tight over her ass and the blouse straining to contain her tits I know I want her. I'm just not sure she's capable of handling all I have to give after eight years in the big house.

Mae: Archer "Justice" Creed may not be completely innocent, but he's not guilty of the crime they convicted him of. Fighting to get him freed was a long, hard battle. What I didn't count on was being attracted to the big, tattooed former lawyer. I know a perfumed rock would look good to him after eight long years in prison, but he's ready and I'm willing. Too bad he's an arrogant asshole out of bed. Unfortunately I ruffled some feathers at the DA's office when I got Justice freed and now I could be in some danger. But do I trust Justice to protect me, or should I go back to Rycks, guardian and an enforcer in Black Reign MC? Our clubs aren't exactly enemies, but they're not friends.

Oh, and those ruffled feathers I mentioned before? They're coming after me. And Justice.

Chapter One

"Archer Creed. Also known as 'Justice.'"

Justice had heard this a thousand times since he went away for murder eight years ago. Usually after he'd beat a motherfucker for pissing him off and some judge was giving him extra time.

This time was different.

"I find myself in the position of being the one to inform you that your conviction has been overturned."

OK. He wasn't expecting that.

"Your lawyer mounted an investigation into the prosecuting attorney for your trial, and there were several… irregularities discovered. While the details of the case are still being hammered out, one thing is certain. Due to prosecutorial misconduct, your conviction is overturned with prejudice."

The judge was an older, balding man with thick glasses and a ruddy complexion. Justice had liked the man on sight, but now Justice wanted to vote him judge of the fucking year. "I haven't reviewed the case because I don't care much, so your lawyer can review the particulars if you want them." He smiled to take the sting out of his words. "I carry out the job the state presents me with. If it doesn't require a judgment from me, I just carry out the order."

He didn't look apologetic at all. Yeah. Justice liked him.

"All I know is the state's attorney overstepped his authority in your case. As such, you cannot be retried for the same crime. The state apologizes for its mistreatment of you."

"I ain't goin' back to that fuckin' place for any reason, judge," Justice said, earning him a frown from the bailiff but a small smile from the judge.

"Can't say that I blame you, son. There are procedures --"

"Ain't. Goin'. Back."

Again, the bailiff frowned, this time putting his hand on his weapon and taking a threatening step forward.

"Stop it, George," the judge said in an exasperated tone. "The man wouldn't be in this position if Alister hadn't fucked up the case in the first damned place."

Justice raised an eyebrow. He'd never heard a judge talk that way in court before. He liked this guy better every second.

The judge turned his attention back to Justice. "I only have one question. After that, you're free to go. The state will send your belongings to the address of your choosing, and you don't have to go collect them yourself."

"Ask," Justice said, crossing his arms over his chest. This ought to be good.

"Why do they call you Justice?"

The question surprised Justice, but only because he expected everyone in the fucking state to know his name. But then, it had been twelve years. "I used to be a lawyer."

"Oh? For what state?"

"Florida." Justice leveled his gaze on the judge. Not backing down an inch.

The older man narrowed his eyes. "Archer Creed…" Then he sat back in his chair, a look of disbelief on his face.

"Don't ask me if I'm *the* Archer Creed or I might just do something to earn that prison sentence."

The judge's previously congenial face hardened. This was the type of judge Justice was used to. "I like you, son. It's the only reason I don't slap you with a contempt charge for that remark." He held Justice's gaze for a moment before speaking again. "I know the case. Was a bit dug into my own business at the time, but I remember thinking they'd hand you your ass for the stunt you pulled."

"You were right."

"Sorry I was. I can't condone violence in any form, but the bastard got what he deserved."

"I only bucked the system, your honor. Bastard had so many people in his pocket, everything I had got thrown out before it could be presented to a jury."

"Ironic that you'd get railroaded into a conviction for a crime you may not have committed in the very case that got you disbarred."

Justice shrugged. "It is what it is."

"I'm surprised your lawyer isn't present for this."

"Far as I know, I don't have one."

"Well, someone took up the cause. Must have a good mind, too, to get that conviction overturned so quickly"

"Quick? If you call eight years quick, you're older than you look."

Surprisingly, that got a sharp bark of laughter from the judge. "Considering the family involved and the fact that Florida doesn't like looking bad in legal matters, yeah. I'd call it quick. Are you telling me you've never met the lawyer who filed this on your behalf?"

"I'm sayin' I didn't know anything was being done on my behalf in the first Goddamned place." Justice glanced at the bailiff. Sure enough, the man winced at his language. There was no way to stop the smirk Justice threw the other man's way. He loved goading easy marks.

The judge had opened his mouth to say something when there was a commotion outside the chamber doors just before they burst open. A short, busty woman in four-inch heels stumbled through the door. She carried a briefcase with several pieces of paper sticking out, and her hair, which probably was supposed to be in a tight bun, was sticking out in several directions in jet-black, kinky curls. No. Curls wasn't exactly right. They wanted to be curls, but they were mostly a frizzy mess. The glasses she wore were too big for her elfin face, her eyes the color of perfect sapphires. She wore a white blouse tucked into a black skirt. The blouse hung from her arms but stretched tightly across her breasts, and her skirt gapped at the waist, but looked like she was barely able to squeeze that generous ass into it. She carried a suit jacket draped over one arm as she caught the door with the other hand to keep from falling. All in all, she was a hot mess.

"Judge Harlan!" She stumbled once more, then righted herself and hurried to the front of the courtroom... to stand beside Justice? What the fuck?

Judge Harlan gave a long-suffering but amused sigh. "Mae Stephens. I should have known you were behind this."

The girl, Mae, hesitated, putting her stuff on the desk in front of her. "Behind what? Did I do something wrong?"

The bailiff snorted. Which kind of pissed Justice off. This Mae couldn't have been much into her twenties and looked as innocent as they came. Right now, she looked confused and unsure of herself.

"No, my dear," Judge Harlan replied immediately. It was the only thing that saved the man from a tongue lashing. Making this girl feel bad had seriously jeopardized his position in Justice's list of favorite people. Short list that it was. "Nothing wrong. It's just that you always seem to show up in the middle of unusual cases. Always the one working to free someone from prison."

"Well, innocent people shouldn't be locked up. And Mr. Creed was innocent."

"Not sure about that, Miss Stephens. But you did uncover some pretty massive problems within the DA's office. A word of advice, though, and I mean this in the most sincere way possible. You're a good girl. I don't want to see you hurt." He glanced at Justice, and Justice got the impression he wanted him to pay attention to what he had to say as much as he wanted Mae to. "You've made some powerful people look bad. Cost one of them his livelihood and another one his freedom. Lay low for a while. Don't work on any more Innocence Projects for a while, or whatever it is you do. This one could very well cost you more than you're willing to pay."

Yeah. Justice got the message loud and clear.

"If that's true," Mae said, regaining her confidence, "it's no more than they deserve. They broke the law just as much as they said Mr. Creed did. And by giving him a life sentence, they took his life away just as much as they said he took the life of someone else. At least he allegedly did it for the right reasons. Vigilantism isn't a good thing, but sometimes it's all the little people have."

Judge Harlan sighed. "You're too much of an idealist for your own good, Mae. Just… be careful. I like you very much and don't want to have to preside over someone accused of hurting you."

Mae shook her head. "You won't, sir. You're too

good a judge not to recuse yourself if it comes to that."

"Are you for fuckin' real?" Justice couldn't hold back any longer.

She jumped and actually took a few steps away from him. Those eyes of hers were big and wide and so fucking blue he swore they were fathomless pools of water. "I-I'm just... that is, I'm o-only... Judge Harlan would never..."

Justice looked to the judge and put his hands on his hips. "You've got to be fuckin' kiddin' me."

The judge gave him a stern look. "You owe her, Justice. She had no clue the nest she was poking in when she started this, I'm sure. You know."

The fuck he did know. The DA's office was littered with dirty lawyers with cops in their pockets. They'd made this town their own and had no intention of giving up the power they'd so skillfully obtained. If little Mae here had managed to get his sentence overturned, then that power was seriously breached. They'd want retribution.

"Damned straight I know! What the fuck?"

"Just do the right thing."

"Fucker," Justice mumbled. The damned man knew he could no more leave this girl on her own than he could quit breathing.

"Well. Now that's settled, I can officially reprimand you, Miss Stephens. You do not barge into my courtroom during a session. I think you know this."

"I'm sorry, your honor. I had trouble at the door."

"Forgot to remove your gun and knife from your briefcase again?"

Justice perked up. What did he just say? And why did it make his cock stir with interest? Scratch that last. He'd just come out of eight years in prison with no women. A perfumed rock would probably turn him on at this point.

"And the pepper spray," she muttered. "Sorry."

Judge Harlan exchanged a look with Justice. The older man looked quite amused. Whether at Mae's situation or Justice's, he didn't know. Justice's head was spinning, and his stomach clenched. He had the feeling he was in for the ride of his life with this chick.

"Just try not to let it happen again, Miss Stephens. Now. I've already given Mr. Creed the good news he's being set free. Did you have anything to add?"

"He's not going back to prison for any reason," she said vehemently. "I would respectfully request you have the facility mail his belongings to the address of his choice."

"Not sure I can do that," the judge said, scratching his chin thoughtfully. "Procedures, you know."

"Sir! You can't send him back! He's already been locked up for *eight years*! Making him go back on a procedural matter would be tantamount to torture! To say nothing of the possibility he could be murdered by a murderous mob!"

"Murdered by a murderous mob, huh?" The judge grinned.

"Exactly!"

Mae looked every bit as horrified as she might have if it had been her facing additional time in prison because of some stupid rules. Justice admired her passion. And the fact that her breathing had sped up. Her breasts now threatened to test the buttons on her blouse. It would represent the first pair of titties he'd seen in eight years, and he was eager to see what they'd look like. He must have licked his lips while looking at them because Judge Harlan cleared his throat several times.

Justice looked up at him. "What?"

"None of that."

"I didn't do anything."

Mae looked at him, confused. "Don't do anything to get thrown back in jail," she hissed. "I've almost got you free."

Justice didn't have the heart to tell her it had already been decided.

"Miss Stephens, while I admire your passion, wasn't it procedural issues that got this man freed? Would you want to go against them now that you got what you wanted?"

She just blinked at the older man. "I, uh... well, no. But..."

"Relax, Mae. He's not going back."

She glared at the judge. "Then why --"

"Because you're fun to tease. Now. Anything else?"

"We'd like to seek damages," she blurted out. "Eight years of his life is a lot to make up for."

"I'm sure you will, and I have no doubt you'll win a substantial amount. In fact, I suggest you stick close to Mr. Creed until you have all the details worked out."

"I'll be working closely with him, your honor."

"Closer than you did while he was in prison, I hope. Seriously. Stick close to him. He was a brilliant lawyer. I'm sure he could help you. Especially given you're not actually a lawyer yourself. He'll help you with those pesky procedures." He placed his hands on his desk and stood. "If there's nothing else, I'll consider this matter closed. Make sure the court has your address, Mr. Creed. Make a list of your belongings, and the court will make sure the state returns them." He banged the gavel. "Court adjourned."

Justice turned to Mae, looking her up and down once more. She was a little disheveled, but the more he looked at her, the more he liked what he saw. But, Christ, she was young. Too damned young for the likes of him. Looking down at her upturned face now -- no makeup, a smattering of freckles across her cheeks -- he wondered if she was actually out of her teens.

"If you're not a lawyer, what are you?"

She stiffened. "Just a concerned citizen who knows how to read. I thought I might go to law school one day, but I haven't managed to get in. Yet."

He tilted his head to the side. "Why not?"

She shrugged. "I'm not very good at taking tests."

"I see. Well, we'll see what we can do about that. Let's get outta here."

Taking her arm, Justice steered her out of the courtroom and outside the building. "Where's your car? We'll swing by the clubhouse, then I'll take you to lunch." Something in the back of his mind worried Justice. Mae Stephens. The name was familiar, but he couldn't place it. Likely because every time he looked at her his gaze dropped to either her tits or her ass.

"Um, I don't have a car." She looked slightly ashamed. "Sorry. I didn't think to call one for you."

"You got a phone?"

"Yes," she said, slipping it out of her purse and handing it to him. He punched in Thorn's number, following her when she started walking to the parking lot.

"Thought you said you didn't have a car."

"I don't." She said it in almost a singsong voice.

Thorn answered the phone just as Mae reached her ride, and Justice was speechless.

"Listen, you little motherfucker," Thorn said, irritated that Justice hadn't spoken when he'd answered. "I don't know who the fuck you are, but I'll track this fuckin' call and fuck you the fuck up."

"It's me," Justice said. "I'll call you back."

"The hell you will! Where the fuck are you?"

"At the courthouse. Goin' home. Open the house." He ended the call, hoping Thorn understood that he was going home and to have someone open the place up and maybe get some groceries and shit.

"What the fuck do you think you're doin'?"

Mae stopped mid-way through putting on a helmet. She'd stuffed her briefcase in a backpack -- after putting to rights the papers sticking out -- and slung the thing over her shoulders.

"Putting my helmet on?"

"Where's your car?" This was not computing.

"I told you. I don't have one." She gestured to the bike. "It's easier to find a parking spot with my bike."

"You've got to be fuckin' kiddin' me." Justice thrust her phone at her. While she put it the side pocket of her backpack, he slung his leg over her bike, starting it and revving the engine a couple of times. "Fuckin' piece of shit," he muttered. "Why did I have to get a hard-on for a piece of shit bike like this fuckin' thing?" Because, really. Had she driven a hybrid or even some kind of muscle car, he'd have been able to ignore her appeal. Not with her riding a bike. "How do you even ride it with those ridiculous shoes?"

"It has an aftermarket electric shifter. Keeps my shoes from getting scuffed at the toe."

"Fuck," he muttered, checking everything out,

not paying Mae a bit of attention. Rather, trying not to. The more he was around her, the more he realized she was fucking sex in a tight skirt and fuck-me heels.

"Get on," he snapped.

"That's my bike!"

"Yeah, but I ain't ridin' bitch. Get on."

* * *

Hadn't Rycks warned her not to go anywhere with this guy? How the hell did she end up on the back of her own bike with him taking her God knows where without putting up a fight?

To be fair, Archer "Justice" Creed was quite possibly the hottest guy she'd ever seen. And, living in the Black Reign compound for so many years, she'd seen quite a bit. She and Rycks had had a contentious relationship for a long time. He'd always picked on her, laughed at her just shy of being cruel to her. He'd done the same with Lucy, but she'd told him off more often than not. Not since Mae'd been kidnapped, though. The experience had been the most terrifying of her life. One she had no desire to relive for any reason. Since then, Rycks had mostly sheltered and coddled her and the other girls he'd taken in, so she was sure this guy would do something soon to piss her off. Like comment on her wide ass or her humongous tits. Or tell her that, no, she couldn't have another kitten. Because, seriously. How many kittens were too many? Since Rycks had brought her home after that horrendous time, he'd given her anything and everything she'd wanted. The man who'd once taunted and tested her had instead protected her like she was his own daughter. So, once Justice denied her any little thing she mentioned she wanted, her temper would kick in, and she'd snag her pepper spray and squirt him in the eyes. Rycks would be proud of her, and she'd regain her sanity.

Currently, they were flying down the highway, weaving their way between cars at an alarming speed. Fortunately, Justice handled the bike even better than Rycks did. After an eight-year absence from riding, that was saying something. When they came to a more congested section of road and had to stop at a light, she tapped his shoulder.

"Aren't we going a touch fast? You just got out of jail. I'm sure you don't want to get a speeding ticket."

"I promise you, I'm in control of this bike. If you're afraid I'll cause you to get hurt, I'm telling you I won't."

"OK, first of all, you don't know that. Secondly, it's a matter of the law. You're breaking the speed limit."

He gave her a cocky grin that made her stomach flip. "Honey, breakin' the law's what I do." He revved the engine a couple more times, then took off again. Thank goodness she had her arms firmly around his waist. For more than one reason. Had she ever felt a more solid set of abs? Made her want to tunnel her hand under his shirt and feel what was under there.

Finally, after what seemed like an hour, they pulled into the driveway of a small house. A bike had just pulled out, a man and a woman seated on it. The man threw up a hand at Justice but didn't stop. Justice turned off the bike and held Mae's arm, steadying her as she got off.

"Why'd you get this piece of shit? You gonna ride, get a Harley."

"'Cause I like speed."

Justice chuckled. "Yeah, I bet you do." He looked at her up and down, assessing her. "Come on inside. I'll change clothes, grab my wallet, then we'll get something to eat."

"Why didn't you just say so? I could have taken you someplace good several miles back. Tito's Diner is the best place in Palm Springs to eat. Besides, I need to see Elena. She made the most delicious pie for my birthday, and I need to thank her."

"Yeah, Tito's is the best. Let me change into something a little less orange and we'll go."

Her hands flew up to her cheeks, embarrassment scalding her. "Oh! I totally wasn't thinking! I'm so sorry!" Of course, he'd want to change out of his prison clothes. She was such an idiot!

He shrugged. "Come on in. Stryker and Glitter opened the place up to air it out. Probably put some food and fresh linens away. Hopefully some beer."

"You can't drink and ride my bike."

"Didn't plan on it, sugar. We'll take my bike when we leave."

"Uh, you'll take your bike. I'll take mine."

"Oh, now. Your sweet ass is goin' behind mine. You heard the judge. You're gonna have people after you, and I'm stayin' on you like stink on shit." He grabbed her hand and tugged her toward the house. "Come on. I want a shower and a change of clothes. You can wash my back."

When he winked at her, Mae's mouth went dry. She wasn't prepared for him to flirt with her. In retrospect, she probably should have been. The man had been in prison for a long damned time. Of course, he'd want to get laid. Rolling that over in her mind, she found she wasn't really opposed to the idea. While she wasn't free with her sexuality, she didn't mind having a little fun now and then. Though, with this guy it probably wasn't the smartest thought.

But, Jesus, he was gorgeous! Big muscles.

Tattoos. And, God, the beard! His hair was shaggy, and that full beard was sprinkled with gray, but he was absolutely stunning with his bad-boy vibe practically sending out mating calls every time he moved. She'd been around hot men most of her life. Lived with them in that clubhouse at Black Reign. But never had a man looked more gorgeous to her. Maybe it was the fact that she'd done nothing but live and breathe his case for the last couple of years, but she felt a territorial pull toward him. She wanted to mark him for her own.

Right. As if a man like him would accept her claim. But did it really matter? All in good fun, right? Live for the moment. Did she dare?

Justice disappeared into the bathroom, leaving the door open. The second he tossed out the orange top and bottoms, followed closely by socks and underwear, Mae's mind was made up. No way she was missing out on this.

She slipped off her heels, then her blouse and skirt. She was unhooking her bra when Justice stepped out of the bathroom into the hallway and met her gaze. She froze with her hands at the front clasp of her bra like a naughty child caught with her hand in the cookie jar. Justice looked her up and down for several seconds, wiping a hand over his mouth. There was something dark and primitive in his gaze. Hot, but he didn't look as if he welcomed what was to come next.

"You ain't usually my type," he muttered. "Too Goddamned innocent. But I ain't lookin' a gift horse in the mouth."

That put her back up. "You know what. Fuck you, Justice." She stopped unhooking her bra and reached for her top. "I thought it'd be fun for both of us, but you're just too much of an asshole." She threaded her arms through the sleeves of the blouse with snappish movements. "I knew better. What the hell was I thinking?"

"Stop." The softly spoken command did something to her. She wanted to comply, but didn't dare. Instead, she paused before resuming.

Mae tried not to look at him, but damn, it was hard. The best she could do was try to forget images of a massive, rock-hard body rippling with muscle and covered in tattoos. Yeah. That wasn't burned into her brain at all.

"I said, stop!" This time he snarled the command, taking the couple of steps separating them and snagging her wrists to keep her from buttoning her top.

"Why would I want to? You don't want me. I supposed that's my innocence shining through because I thought that, after an extended prison sentence, you'd want to fuck." Then a horrifying thought crossed her mind. "U-unless you're gay?" Immediately, she felt her cheeks heat. "Omigod! I'm so sorry! I never thought... That is, I don't know why I didn't consider that you might --"

Justice dragged her to him and silenced her with his mouth on hers. There was nothing soft or coaxing about his domination either. He was bold. Demanding. Sweeping his tongue inside her mouth with the authority of a man who expected to get what he wanted. Mae's knees went weak, and she thought she might have slid to a puddle at his feet if he hadn't circled one arm around her back and held her to him.

God, she could feel those muscles wrapping around her! It was like being in a safe, warm cocoon, only this cocoon was probably more dangerous than the outside world ever thought about being. Mae wasn't stupid. She knew Justice was a violent man. He might actually have killed the people he'd been accused and convicted of killing. And she was going to bed with him.

Well. Bed wasn't exactly where they were headed. Probably the shower. Who knew where after that? One thing was certain, though. She knew this was going to be a life-altering experience.

As her mind started to expand to include more than just his kiss and his strong arms, she realized that his cock was mashed against her belly. The thing was long and thick, pulsating in time with his heart. She knew because she could feel his heart pounding out a hard, steady beat where they were fused together. The only barriers between them currently were her bra and panties, and the open blouse she'd tried to put back on.

The blouse went first. When Mae couldn't get it off fast enough, Justice did it for her. There was a rip of fabric and a grunt from Justice, and the thing just rustled to the floor.

"Lose the bra if you want to keep it," he grunted in between kisses and licks. Somehow she managed, though Justice didn't wait for her to slide her panties down her hips. He tore the waistband so they fluttered down her legs. But there was no time to mourn the loss or scold Justice. He scooped her up and headed to the bathroom and the shower.

He must have started the water while he'd been in there earlier because steam billowed out of the wide stall. She'd been so preoccupied with her own thoughts she hadn't noticed. It wasn't a huge shower by any means, but there was plenty of room for the two of them and a small shelf that could double as a seat on one end.

Opening the glass door, Justice stepped in,

setting her on her feet with him between her and the spray. "Didn't know if you'd join me. Water's probably too hot." He turned and fiddled with it a little before turning around to grab her hand and stick it under the spray. "Too hot?"

She shook her head slightly. "No."

He grinned. "Will be soon."

Mae didn't think he meant the water.

Chapter Two

Justice's head was buzzing with an excessive amount of testosterone. Or at least that was what he was telling himself. There was no possible way this girl was all he was imagining because, if she was, she was likely a goddess. And he damned sure would never be allowed to fuck a goddess.

Her hair was a mass of dark curls that seemed to be everywhere, now damp with the spray from the shower. Her body wasn't lithe and lean, but supple and rounded. Her ass and tits were firm and high, and her waist was so small he could almost span it with his big hands. Her thighs were plump and strong. She wasn't a waif, but a woman built for a hard ride by a man like him.

Not having his arms securely around her wasn't an option for Justice. Not that he wanted to hold her close or that he needed to be in contact with all that impossibly soft skin or anything. No. He just didn't want her to get away from him. Not until he'd fucked her until he passed out. Then she could go wherever she wanted. Maybe.

Pulling her back to him, he buried his face in her neck and inhaled deeply. "Christ, you smell good. Honeysuckle and roses." Had he said that out loud?

She shivered and gave a little whimper, clinging to his shoulders and tilting her head back to give him better access to her neck. Justice took full advantage, licking and nipping the skin there before moving down to her chest.

He shifted her higher in his arms so he could take one nipple into his mouth. The second he did, his eyes widened. Yeah. So fucking goooood! The cries she made, the way she fisted his hair in her little hands, fed his hunger for her. Those thighs he'd admired were now wrapped tightly around him, like an invitation to tuck his cock underneath her body and thrust home. It would take a stronger man than he was to resist her.

Shoving her against the shower wall, he did just that. He slid inside of her like gliding through water. Only this pool was hot and tight, her folds parting almost reluctantly. She cried out and clamped down on him, squirming in his arms. Somehow, Justice managed to stop and assess the situation.

"Steady," he growled. "Breath with me. Am I hurting you?"

"I -- it -- it burns a little."

"You ain't no virgin." He said it as a statement, praying like fuck it was true.

"No. Jus -- just been a while. Give me a second."

"Not sure I can." He bit out the words between clenched teeth and all of a sudden the shower was way too hot. Even with the water pouring down over him, Justice felt his skin break out in a sweat. How the everlasting fuck was he supposed to not move?

Finally, after what seemed like an eternity, Mae nodded, leaning in to kiss him once more. Justice wasn't asking any more questions. He started moving inside her. Gradually, she picked up his movements and rode him, learning his rhythm and matching it perfectly. Soon they were both panting and grinding together. But it wasn't enough for Justice. When he came -- and he was coming soon -- he wanted to do it hard and fast and deep.

Pulling out of her, he set her on the shower floor again, this time spinning her around. "Put your hands on the wall and keep them there," he growled. "Gonna fuck you hard, princess."

"Yes," she panted. "Do it!"

He surged forward once again. This time, he gripped those fleshy globes of her ass in his hands and pulled her back to him. Every thrust was harder until the slapping of skin on skin was loud and hard in the small room. Her cries mingled with his grunts until they were both groaning loudly.

Finally, with a roar, Justice let himself go. Vaguely, he knew he was missing something important, but for the life of him he had no idea what. The whole day seemed to spiral out of control in his mind. The sudden summons to court. The clumsy, sexy girl playing at being a lawyer. The incredible sex. The girl…

Then it all crashed down around him, and Justice came in a pulsating rush of heat and sweat. His cock pulsed and quivered inside Mae, her pussy answering each shudder of his dick with a squeeze and ripple of its own. Mae seemed to gasp for breath, and he found himself pulling her upright, wrapping his arms around her even as he continued to thrust to get out every last drop of cum.

It took a while, but finally both of them were still. Mae still gasped for breath occasionally, but she rested the back of her head against his shoulder and her hands gripped his arms, which were still securely around her.

"You good, princess?"

"Yeah," she sighed. Justice looked down at her. Those big, blue eyes were closed, and a soft, dreamy smile played at her lips. She looked like an angel. So breathtakingly beautiful.

Then reality came crashing in.

He'd just fucked her. Bareback. And he had absolutely no idea who she was or what her agenda was. Or why she'd taken his case on in the first

Goddamned place. Without telling him. In his world, no one did anything without a reason. He just hadn't figured hers out yet.

Justice must have stiffened, because that contented smile faded from Mae's lips and she looked up at him, uncertainty in her gaze.

"What's wrong?"

Justice pulled out of her and turned away, washing himself. "You might want to wash. We'll stop by the pharmacy when we leave." He said it casually. When he turned around, there was this innocent, confused look on her face.

"Pharmacy?"

"Yeah. For the mornin' after pill. Unless you're on something."

Those sapphire eyes widened, then the blood drained from her face and she sat down on the ledge abruptly, as if her legs could no longer hold her up.

"Omigod," she gasped. "How could I have been so stupid?" That last was said on a whisper, as if she, too, had forgotten. Same as he had.

"I'd have thought you'd've been prepared for something like this since you initiated it." Justice tried not to sound too put out, but, honestly, he felt like he'd just been played, but for the first time in his life had no idea what the game was.

"I know," she whispered. "I just got caught up in the moment." She looked up at him. "Do I need to… I don't know. Go to the doctor?"

"You mean, did I fuck around in prison?" He hadn't meant to sound so angry or bitter, but judging by the way she flinched back from him and drew her arms over her chest, that was exactly how he sounded. Which just pissed him off even more. "Little late to cover yourself now, princess. Done fucked your brains out."

"Would you stop belittling me? I made a mistake, OK? I get it! But you were here same as me. And I certainly didn't have to make you get hard, nor did I have to force your dick into my pussy. You did that all on your own. So fuck you, Justice!" She stood and stomped out of the shower... only to slip and nearly fall on her ass. Reflex had Justice grabbing her arm and hauling her back against him. The second her body was next to his again, his cock started to stiffen.

"Oh, no! I gave it up once, but you don't get to do this again. Not after talking to me that way."

"Fuck," he muttered, scrubbing a hand over his face as he let her go once he was sure she had her balance. He needed to apologize. Wanted to, even. But the words just wouldn't form. Mainly because there was something about her nagging at the back of his mind. He should know this girl, but he had no idea where from. He felt he was missing a piece of information here. Shit like that, he didn't trust.

So now he was stuck babysitting a woman who had managed to get him out of a long prison sentence, and he couldn't trust her. Which meant no more fucking her until he figured it out. Just as well. After this debacle she wasn't likely to let him inside that sweet little cunt again any time soon. And fuck it all! He hadn't taken the time to taste it before losing his fucking mind!

Sometimes, life was a bitch, and her stripper name was Karma. At least, he'd heard that somewhere. Maybe.

Fuck.

* * *

The very last thing in the world Mae wanted to do in that moment was get on the back of Justice's bike.

She wanted her own bike. Over her vehement, very loud protest, Justice had refused to give her her keys, or her backpack where her phone was. In fact, he'd threatened to run both her keys and her phone down the garbage disposal if she didn't shut the fuck up about them. She'd had to turn her phone off before entering the courthouse, and he didn't want her turning it back on in case someone was tracking her. Apparently, he was taking all that stuff Judge Harlan had said seriously. She'd missed part of the conversation between Justice and the judge, but Justice said he'd promised he'd protect her until the threat had passed. What threat, she had no idea. No one had threatened her. Besides, Rycks would tear anyone apart looking to harm her.

True to his word, once they'd set out, he stopped by the first pharmacy he came to. Without a word, Mae went inside. Even without the added embarrassment of having to find the item she needed, she was out of sorts. Justice had ripped her blouse enough that he had to put her in one of his T-shirts. She'd knotted it at the waist and put a jacket over it, but she didn't feel like herself.

She looked at the item she needed, Plan B, for a very long time. So long she was afraid she'd start getting funny looks. Placing her hand over her belly, she tried to grasp the gravity of what had happened. It was the first time she'd ever had unprotected sex. That wasn't something she took lightly, but she wasn't certain she wanted to do this. Prevent a pregnancy.

It wasn't that she was opposed to the idea. In certain circumstances, she would be all for it. She just wasn't certain this was one of those times. At least, not for her. She was under no illusion that Justice was the kind of man to stick around and help if she did get pregnant, though she had the feeling he was honorable enough to make sure she and the baby were taken care of. No. If she were pregnant, she had a good support system. No doubt both Rycks and her sister would be disappointed, or at least irritated by her risky behavior, but they'd never abandon her, and they'd always love her and take care of her if she needed it. And, at the moment, watching Rycks beat the shit out of Justice might be more than a little satisfying.

So she walked away, not making that purchase. Instead, she bought a pregnancy test and tucked it quietly away in her jacket pocket where she could keep it until it was needed. If it were needed. She might start her period and all would be well.

When she walked back to Justice and the big Harley he rode, he didn't look at her. Just stared straight ahead or fiddled with the switches and stuff on the console. Once she was seated with her helmet on, he turned his head slightly to speak to her.

"You good?"

"Fine." That got a heavy sigh from him. Apparently, he wasn't as dumb as he acted.

"Still headed to Tito's?"

"My favorite place."

With a grunt, he started the bike and they headed down the road. Mae tried to ignore the fact that riding a bike always made her horny. She also tried to ignore the fact that she didn't have on panties and that she had to spread her legs a little wider on this bike than she did on hers. Because she refused to get any closer to Justice than she absolutely had to, she wasn't as mashed up against his back as she might have been had he been anything other than an asshole after they'd fucked. Unfortunately, that made the wind blow up her skirt and straight to her heated, wet pussy.

Sigh.

Yeah. It was a losing battle. The longer they rode, the hornier she got. Which just pissed her off. By the time they pulled into the parking lot of Tito's, the morning rush was gone and the lunch crowd hadn't started making their way in yet. There were one or two people there, but Mae recognized the bikes and breathed a sigh of relief. Unless she was mistaken, Beast and Thorn were in the diner. Which meant that, even though Justice was Salvation's Bane, they'd make sure she got to stay with her sister, Lucy, until Rycks came for her. It did not, however, relieve her of the temper she'd worked herself into.

The second the bike stopped, she was off, stalking toward the diner as fast as she could in those stupid four-inch heels. If she wasn't so short, she'd never have had to wear them. Which was another thing to add to her already foul mood.

She took all of three steps. On the fourth, she turned her ankle and stumbled several steps before righting herself. And she snapped.

"Fuck!" She screamed the expletive, yanking her shoe off and flinging it as hard as she could across the parking lot. The pavement was already hot, and she had to force herself not to hop as she reached for the other shoe.

"What the fuck do you think you're doin'?" Justice looked even more angry than he had earlier. Right after he'd given her the most splendid orgasm of her life.

"Fuck you, you fucking bastard!" She hurled the shoe at him, end over end like a dagger. He easily batted it out of the air and continued toward her.

Mae ignored him. She turned and marched into the diner. Tito raised a hand to her in greeting, his always pleasant and charming smile working to coax her from her bad mood.

"Hey, little Mae," he said cheerily. "Glad I'm not the one to make you so angry you lose your footwear. My Elena would kick my ass if it was." His lightly accented English was always soothing. Even though she wanted to stay angry, she couldn't help but relax a little.

"You good, Mae?" Thorn stood, moving to her just as Justice stormed inside the diner.

"What the fuck, Mae? You'll burn your feet on the fuckin' blacktop!"

"Don't you say another word to me, asshole!"

Of course, Justice ignored her, grabbing her upper arm lightly and tugging her after him. Mae struggled, but refrained from using too much more bad language. Elena and Marge were saints, but they would tolerate only so much before they shut them all down.

The diner was set up so the long counter was the center of the place. The booths were lined up against the outside wall, forming a single horseshoe around the counter. Behind the counter, which Tito constantly manned, were the grill and cook stations. Justice shoved her gently into the booth in the front corner of the diner, probably because he had a view of everyone except Marge in the back. Sure enough, once Mae settled, she saw Thorn and Beast headed their way from across the room. Both men looked puzzled, their gazes shifting warily from her to Justice and back. Justice inclined his head at them both in greeting.

"Everything OK here?" As president, Thorn took the lead in the conversation.

"Yes," Justice said at the same time Mae said, "No!"

Justice glared at her, to which Mae narrowed her eyes. "You threatening me? Because, let me tell you, I've faced down worse men than you. Takes more than a scowl to scare me."

Marge came to the table, a tall glass of some yummy-looking ice-cream concoction on her tray, along with three beers. "Looks like someone needs a Marge special," she said, setting the ice cream down in front of Mae, flashing her a concerned smile. Marge set two of the beers down in front of the Salvation's Bane members before turning to Justice. "Glad to see you again. Even happier to see you're free. It's why you get this." She set the beer on the table in front of him harder than strictly necessary, causing the golden liquid to slosh over the side slightly. "Don't mean you get a pass to be an asshole to little Mae, though. Whatever you did, apologize or this is the last service you get in this diner." She walked away with a swish of her narrow hips and a toss of her head, which didn't move the red Beehive hairdo. For the briefest of moments, Mae thought she saw a look of disappointment on Justice's face before he once again brought down that hard mask.

"We have a situation," Justice said to Thorn, ignoring Mae.

"I see that. Might want to take her home, 'cause she don't seem too happy with your company."

"No," Justice said at the same time Mae said, "Yes, please!"

Mae gave Justice a withering glare before turning to Thorn. "Could I please use your phone? Or, better yet, just text Lucy and tell her to have Rycks pick me up here."

Justice's head snapped around so he faced her. "What the fuck does he have to do with this?" Then his eyes widened, and his mouth opened. "Well, fuck me raw."

"Too fucking late," she snapped back at him.

"OK." Beast held up his hands. "What the hell's goin' on here?"

Mae and Justice just stared daggers at each other, neither backing down an inch.

"Mae pissed off some pretty powerful people in the city when she got my conviction overturned," Justice began, totally misinterpreting the question Beast asked. Likely on purpose.

"Figured." Thorn nodded. "She's nothing if not thorough at proving her beliefs. In this case, it just happened that the DA's office was full to overflowing with corruption."

"I was gonna take the fall regardless," Justice said, looking at Mae. "My watch. My responsibility."

"Wait," she said, rubbing her forehead. "You let them convict you... on purpose?" He just looked at her, and Mae wanted to scratch his handsome face with eight bloody furrows. "That's the stupidest thing I've ever heard!"

"Watch your mouth," he snapped. "You have no idea what you're talkin' about so just shut up and listen."

"Justice," Thorn said quietly. "The girl did the impossible. You might show some gratitude."

He smirked. "Already did."

"Fuck you," she muttered, trying to scoot him over so she could get out and leave the diner. When he didn't move, she stood on the seat and was in the process of climbing over the back when Justice snagged her and put her back in the seat.

"Stay where I put you."

"Hey!" Beast snapped. "She ain't a dog, bro."

"No, but she's behaving like a naughty child."

"Says the man having his own temper tantrum. Why not tell them why you're really upset? 'Cause, quite frankly, I'd like to know my own fucking self." She slid a glance over to a frowning Tito and winced. She mouthed, "Sorry." He just nodded and focused on Justice.

"Really? Why don't you tell them? My version won't be so soft and sweet." Yeah. He'd totally called her bluff on that one. No way she was saying anything to anyone except maybe Lucy. Maybe.

Thorn looked from one of them to the other, his eyes widening. "Oh, hell no!" He took out his phone, stabbed it a couple of times, then put it to his ear. "Yeah. Need you at Tito's. Bring an extra helmet." Then he hung up. "Justice, get your ass outta here. Now. I'll hand her off to Rycks. Black Reign can take it from here."

Justice crossed his arms over his chest. "She's my responsibility. I promised Judge Harlan I'd protect her."

"Then fuckin' do it from afar! She's goin' with Rycks and that's my final say."

"Don't want to spend my first day outta prison arguing with you, Thorn."

"Then don't!"

"But she's not leavin' my side. Not until we make sure any threat to her is under wraps. That ain't happenin' anytime soon."

"Look. You know Rycks has taken her as his ward along with several other girls. That man guards them with his fuckin' life. He was against her goin' to court today, but apparently" -- he gave Mae a withering look --"she snuck out. He finds out the two of you've been... gettin' to know each other, he'll kill you."

"I can fuckin' take care of myself," Justice snapped. He looked over at Marge, who had her arms crossed, watching intently, with an angry scowl on her face. "Would you mind bringin' Mae something to eat? It's past lunch, and I'd bet my last day as a free man on this earth that she skipped breakfast this morning."

"Did not," she muttered.

"Coffee don't count." To Mae's utter annoyance, Justice and Thorn said it at the same time.

"You don't know me," she spat at Justice. "You don't get a say."

"Honey, I was a lawyer. We live on coffee same as military. I recognize the look. When was the last time you had more than coffee for breakfast?" When she just sat there, he nodded crisply. "What I thought."

As always, Marge didn't ask what she wanted. She just brought a big stack of pancakes with bacon, a tall glass of milk, and a cup of black coffee. She had only finished half the milkshake, so Mae slid it to the side. Might be able to drink it later, but probably not. Justice raised his eyebrows at the amount of maple syrup she put on the pancakes, but said nothing.

Mae cut a forkful and stuffed it in her mouth. She grinned at Justice. The longer he sat there, the more entertainment for her. She ate contentedly until about half her stack was gone. Beyond full didn't quite cover how she was feeling, but hey. They'd quit talking about Rycks and Justice getting out of there and started talking about all the people she'd pissed off. She'd known the list was long and distinguished, but, if Thorn was right, she might be in a bit more trouble than she'd figured on. Rycks would have it covered, though. He could protect her better than anyone else.

Speak of the devil. Rycks came flying into the

parking lot of the diner. Surprisingly, he wasn't riding one of the little crotch-rockets he'd taught her to love, but a big-ass Harley with all the loud, rattling pipes. He pulled up to the door sideways, obviously preparing for a quick getaway, then stormed into the small diner.

His eyes found hers immediately, but he did a sweep of the rest of the diner before settling on Justice. "Mae, get on the bike."

She made to move, but Justice draped his arm around her shoulders, holding her in place. Beast groaned, closing his eyes in resignation. Thorn just sat back, hands over his chest, prepared to watch.

"Not in my diner!" Tito yelled. "Out with all-a-ya!" He turned to Mae. "Except you, little Mae. you stay with me and Elena. Us and Marge will protect you."

Rycks said nothing, his gaze locked on Justice, his eyes narrowing. Finally, he nodded. "OK. I see. What are you going to do about it?"

Justice just shrugged. "Ain't decided."

That was the wrong answer. Rycks lunged for him. Justice dodged him, but managed to drag Mae out of the booth with him, keeping her behind him, one arm managing to hold her in place.

"I'll take care of her, Rycks. I gave my word and I break it for no one."

"She's my ward. She made the decision to stay with me over her sister because she knows I'm the best there is to protect her. I've been doing it a long time."

"Do you know the threat to her? What she brought down on herself by takin' on my case?"

"I do."

"Then why the fuck'd you let her do it?" Now Justice sounded angry enough to kill someone.

Probably Rycks.

"Because it was important to her. And you didn't deserve to rot in prison for something you didn't do."

"I was the enforcer for Salvation's Bane. It was my job to take the fall if the club came under scrutiny."

"Yeah, but you never looked into why things went down the way they did. I hate to tell you, my friend, but you have a rat inside your club. You took care of the original one, but this new one's very personal."

Chapter Three

There was complete silence while they all processed Rycks's words. Finally, Thorn stood.

"Go to the clubhouse."

"No," Rycks said immediately. "Not this time. You want this information, you come to me." He reached out his hand for Mae. "Come on."

Mae moved, but Justice tightened his grip on her. "She stays with me."

"Do you really have time for this?" Rycks snapped. Justice had never met the man personally, but he had a reputation of being as cool and levelheaded as El Diablo. This show of temper didn't sit well with Justice at all.

"Don't know. But she's still not goin' anywhere without me."

"You can follow. No one said you couldn't."

"Not good enough."

Rycks focused on Mae. "Do you feel safe with him?"

Mae looked from one to the other. Did she? "Well, yeah, but --"

Rycks cut her off. "Fine. But you bring her to the Black Reign compound. Thorn, if you want to get a group together to join us, it would be preferable. I've got Black Reign riding in force to meet us and escort us in."

"Sounds pretty serious," Thorn mused.

"Because it is."

"Why'd you let her do this?" Justice demanded. "If you knew it would carry this much fallout, why let her do it?"

"Honestly? I never thought she'd find as much as she did. She's highly intelligent and like a pit bull when she's on to something. I just never figured she'd be able to uncover the massive amount of corruption inside the DA's office. Hell, we didn't know it ourselves. How they kept it a secret for so long is beyond me. Not with so many people involved. Besides, like I said. You weren't the one who should have been in prison." He backed off, moving to the door. Rycks's gaze scanned the parking lot and the road beyond it. "We need to go. Now."

"Got everyone close by comin' to meet us," Thorn said. "We're gonna stick out like a beat dick."

"Better than being vulnerable," Rycks said. "The more attention we draw, the less likely they are to strike. They don't like attention."

"Noted," Thorn grunted.

Justice snagged Mae's hand and headed out the door.

"I'm sorry, Tito," Mae said over her shoulder.

"He don't make this right, little Mae, you let me know," Tito called after her.

Justice scooped her up and carried her to his bike. "Helmet," Justice snapped, tossing it to her when they reached it and he sat her on it. This was fucking madness. He'd thought the killing years earlier had been from one of the guy's victims and was prepared to fight it out, but then the case had started to snowball on him. Piece after piece of evidence leading the investigation straight to Bane's door. Once that happened, Justice had no other option. He took the hit to keep the cops out of Bane's business.

"Don't think this is the end of this --"

"It is. Hang on, princess."

Justice knew he'd fucked up. He also knew he was serious about not letting her leave his side. And if she thought he didn't know she hadn't bought the contraceptive, she wasn't as smart as she thought she was. Ten to one she bought a pregnancy test instead. What he still hadn't worked out was why. That would have to take a back seat to the more immediate threat. While he hadn't ruled out that she was the bait in some elaborate trap to take him down, he hadn't yet figured out the reason. Somehow, that explanation didn't fit. He was pretty sure Rycks wouldn't allow it, and Mae's sister was Vicious's ol' lady. If the target had been Justice, they'd have tried something in prison. Any attempts there had been amateurish by his standards, and easily fought off. It didn't make sense someone would target him enough to use Mae to this extent. No. She wanted something else from him. But what?

It wasn't long before they were all riding down the highway, taking as many back roads as they could to Lake Worth and the Black Reign compound. Several of Salvation's Bane joined them, forming a wall around Justice and Mae. When the riders from Black Reign joined them for the last few miles, they did the same, shoring up any weak points around the couple. It set Justice's teeth on edge. He did the protecting. Not the other way around.

Justice had to admit, the second they pulled into the compound parking lot, he was officially impressed. The clubhouse was massive. Three stories with balconies top to bottom. A huge garage was open, with five bays filled with bikes. Some were parked, others being worked on or serviced in some way. He could tell there were more buildings behind the two massive structures, but was unable to identify what they were. Yeah. This club had money. Likely all from El Diablo.

One by one, the guys shut off their bikes, and the place seemed eerily silent. Justice glanced back at Mae. She had a smug little smile on her face like he was the butt of a joke he didn't yet get. He gave her a warning glance, but said nothing. He climbed off carefully, aware she hadn't retrieved her shoes. The drive was concrete, but he still didn't want to risk her burning her feet, so he scooped her up.

"What the hell do you think you're doing?" She squirmed, struggling to get down, but Justice just carried her toward the clubhouse, following Rycks. The other man scowled at him over his shoulder.

"Makin' sure you don't burn your fuckin' feet, princess." That calmed her down. She still didn't slide her arms around his neck. Not that he cared. At all.

Once they were up on the wraparound porch, he set her down. She stepped away from him immediately and stormed inside. Justice shook his head and followed her at a more leisurely pace. Rycks was already inside talking to El Segador in hushed tones. The rest of the club in the room stood around the room, facing the door, at the ready. More than one fingered a gun at his hip.

Club girls draped themselves artfully on the stair rails along the second-story landing. Some of them eyed him blatantly, while others whispered amongst themselves. All of them looked over the men from Salvation's Bane as they entered the common room.

Thorn strode right up to Rycks and El Segador without hesitation. "OK, Rycks. We're here. What's so fuckin' important it couldn't have been discussed in neutral territory?"

Rycks glanced at Thorn, then his features hardened. Justice had seen that look many times. A fight was about to happen, and Justice knew he was the target.

He glanced around to find Mae to make sure she was out of the way. Thankfully, she was a good way away, her arms crossed, a look equal parts satisfaction and trepidation on her face. As if she were trying to convince herself she was looking forward to the confrontation.

The second he looked back, Rycks was on him, slamming his fist into Justice's face twice in rapid succession. With a growl, Justice launched his own attack, landing punches in Rycks's side before dropping his shoulder and tackling the guy to the floor. Whoops and cheers came from the men surrounding them. Justice thought he heard a couple of Bane's members yelling him on, but he wasn't sure.

For several minutes, the fight was intense. Both men scored blood but neither seemed to be able to get the upper hand. Rycks fought like mad, but his expression didn't hold the fierceness Justice expected from a man out to kill him. Lord knew, as many times as men had been out to end him in prison, Justice knew what it looked like. No. Rycks was out to make an example of Justice. No one fucked with Mae and got away clean. Justice got it.

With a heavy sigh, Justice backed away and put his arms down, ready to just hunker down and take it. Rycks didn't disappoint. Instantly, he was on Justice, knowing there was blood in the water and that he could do what he needed.

Rycks beat Justice until he was on the floor protecting his head and nothing else. The beating continued for another few seconds before Rycks backed off, breathing heavily, looking down his nose at the other man. Justice braced himself on one elbow, spat blood, then looked up at Rycks.

"Feel better now?"

Rycks looked over at Mae. Justice followed his gaze and saw the little princess standing ramrod straight, her fists clenched at her sides. Her face was pale and her lips thin. Her attention was on Justice, but when she realized he was looking at her, she quickly found Rycks. She gave a very slight nod before dropping her gaze. Rycks walked to Justice and extended his hand. Justice took it and let the other man help him to his feet. He'd fucked up. He got it.

"If you're serious about protecting her until this thing is done, you're welcome here."

"I'm not leaving without her. If you won't let me take her back to Palm Springs with me, then I have no other choice." Justice wanted it known to everyone he was serious. His own club included. Much as he hated being away from them now he was out of prison, he wasn't about to break his word first time out. Besides, there was unfinished business between him and Mae.

"Fine. But just so we're clear." Rycks stepped close to Justice, death in his eyes. "Mae, Winter, and Serilda are daughters of my heart. You fuck with any of them, you fuck with me."

"You made that abundantly clear." Justice was fairly certain the man had broken a rib as well as his nose. Hard to not understand that.

"We may revisit this. I've not had the opportunity to find out from Mae exactly what went down, but she'll confide in me eventually. When she does, we may have more to… discuss."

"If you're her guardian, then it's your right. If she were my daughter, I'd feel the same."

Rycks gave him a nod, then went to Mae. He spoke softly to her, and she nodded, taking a deep breath. She still looked visibly shaken, but not like she was about to lose her shit.

"Mae, take Justice to a room and let him get settled. He'll probably want to clean up."

She nodded, not saying anything but looking at Justice with something close to shame in her gaze. Yeah. The woman knew she was the reason for his beat down and wasn't sure how to feel about it. Interesting. Not that he cared.

Mae let him to the second floor, halfway down the hall, and opened a room with a stripped-down bed, a dresser, and a couch in front of a TV. Like the rooms on the front side, the back had a balcony overlooking the property. It was a nice room by any standards, but Justice just crossed his arms over his chest and refused to go inside.

"What?" she demanded, her voice lacking the snippiness she was probably going for.

"That your room?"

"I'm just across the hall." She walked to the other door and opened it. This time, Justice strode the width of the hallway and straight into her space. "What do you think you're doing?" Now she sounded appropriately snippy. Justice found himself fighting a grin.

"Where you go, I go. Not staying in a different room. You're glued to my side for the foreseeable future, princess."

"No. Hell, no." She shook her head almost violently. "You're not sleeping in here with me."

He shut and locked the door, walking around the large space, checking the windows and the balcony door. The locks were high end and tied to the security system. She was definitely protected from intruders, and he doubted she could get out without alerting someone else. All were encouraging.

"Didn't say I was sleeping with you. I'll sleep on the floor if you prefer. But I'm definitely sleeping in this room. As close to you as I can get."

"Look, Justice. No one can get in here, and I'm not sneaking out. I get the danger, and I'm glad everyone is taking it seriously. But I don't want you in my private space."

"You heard Rycks. Unless you go tell him why you don't want me in your room, you're stuck with me." Justice shrugged as if it made no difference to him at all, when, in fact, it could be the difference between him being with her and Rycks forcibly kicking them all out.

She bit her lip and looked out the window. "Fine," she said softly. "On the floor, then. Or the couch. Whatever. Just not in my bed."

"Wouldn't think of it, princess." He winked at her, belying what he'd just said. He would definitely be thinking about it. He hoped she would be as well.

* * *

Most of the time, Mae missed her sister like she'd miss her right arm. At times like this, she thought she'd go mad without her. She'd asked Rycks to see if Thorn would get Vicious to bring Lucy to visit, but with Lucy being pregnant, Vicious was understandably reluctant to bring his woman into what they considered a rival clubhouse.

As she sat in the common room, Justice lounging on the couch beside her, she found she needed to know what the plan was. What the end goal was. When her life could get back to normal.

"We need to talk," she said softly.

"Wondered when you'd tell me that." He downed the beer he'd been nursing for the past half hour and stood, holding out his hand to her. "Come on."

Mae hesitated a second before placing her hand in his. Those warm, strong fingers closed around her hand and she wanted to melt. She tried to pull away out of sheer self-preservation, but when he hung on, she gave up.

Justice took her upstairs to her room and closed and locked the door. Leading her to the couch, he urged her to sit, then sat beside her, putting his arm around her. For long moments they sat like that. Mae was equally turned on and utterly miserable.

"What's going to happen to me?"

"Nothing. You're going to be inconvenienced for a few weeks. Maybe less. Then life will go on as normal."

She turned to him. "How can you say that? Even Rycks is freaking out about this. That man does not freak out."

"It's a serious situation, and he cares about you. Any father would react this way about his daughter."

"Then why did he let me do it to begin with?" If she were honest, that was the real reason she was upset. Either Rycks hadn't thought she was capable, or he'd had no idea what she was really getting into. Neither was a good answer for her. Maybe she suffered a case of hero worship with Rycks, but she really thought he knew everything going on in this town.

Justice sighed. "Didn't you hear him before?"

"I did, but it doesn't make sense."

"He thought you'd find out enough to overthrow my conviction, but never dreamed you'd stumble onto the vipers' nest you did." When she looked away from him, Justice grasped her chin and turn her head back to him. "We all know the justice department in Palm Springs is rotten from the top down. There are hands in everything from tax evasion to securities fraud, to racketeering, to drug deals, and any number of bottom-of-the-barrel scum you can imagine. It's been that way for a long time. No one has ever been able to link specific crimes to specific people the way you did with the DA and me. Had it not been for me being convicted, you'd never have gone digging, and the people you singled out would never have been found out, let alone paid for any of their crimes. Not only did you get the DA disbarred, but he and three other people are going up on federal charges that will likely land them in prison for the rest of their lives. You did that, princess."

Why did that nickname send shivers through her? And he could use it as a caress or a sneer at his choosing. She much preferred the caress. Though she'd never tell him that. Whatever she was feeling ran one way.

"Are you guys working on figuring out how much trouble I'm in?"

"You know we are. I've got your six, and I have my ways of knowing what's going on. Always have. So, even though it doesn't seem like I know what's going on with Reign's investigation, I do."

She looked away again, unexpectedly near tears. The questions she needed to ask him, she couldn't. Not only did he not know she'd not taken the pill, but there was no way to bridge that gap. Not after Rycks beat the crap out of him on her behalf. One cheek was swollen, and he had several cuts on his face. Probably was hurt more than he wanted to admit.

"Why don't you ask what's really on your mind, princess?"

She stood. "That's all that's on my mind. I just want my life to get back to normal and for you to be out of it." She sounded snippy, but there was no other way for her to say it without bursting into tears. Rycks had done a lot to make her feel safe and wanted, but she was beginning to believe only he and Lucy really wanted her around.

"Regrettin' gettin' me out of a tight spot?"

"No." It was the truth. He was rapidly becoming a thorn in her side, but she couldn't regret her actions on his behalf. "It was the right thing to do."

"But it didn't have to be you." Justice said it softly, and it felt like a caress.

"Yes. It did. The others were too close. Any number of them could have become a target. I had no idea why you'd let them have you, but I figured it had something to do with honor or a code among bikers. Rycks tried to keep me out of it, but he felt the same way I did." She started pacing slowly in front of the couch, trying to think things through. "Since Rycks and a few of the guys from Salvation's Bane rescued me a few years back, Rycks has been a father figure. I can't explain how it's not creepy or anything, but me and Winter and Serilda have been under his protection. And, believe me, he can be vicious about it."

"Oh, you don't have to tell me about that, darlin'. Got the proof all over my fuckin' body."

That got a surprised giggle from her. "Sorry," she said, clearing her throat. He just grinned and indicated she should continue. "Anyway, in all that time, he's never let us put ourselves in danger. I mean, he even insists we wear our seat belts, and God forbid we should get a speeding ticket. He lets us ride bikes, but only with the proper gear."

"Guessing that little skirt and those fuck-me shoes don't count as proper attire?"

She felt the blood rush to her cheeks as she admitted, "No. And the only reason he's not called me out on it is because of this whole situation. Believe me, he noticed. He's just choosing his battles. He'll bring it up later, though. Don't worry."

"Go on."

"Well, after all that, he let me go after your conviction. Not once did he warn me off. Now I have to ask myself if he was using me to get something he wanted, and I feel horrible about even thinking it."

Justice was silent for a long time after that. So much so that Mae met his gaze, afraid she'd see anger but just as afraid she'd see indifference. Was she that disposable? She had been to everyone but Lucy until Rycks. Had he now found his use for her and damn her safety if it got him what he needed? If that were true, why was he so concerned about Justice? Justice wasn't Black Reign.

"Come here, Mae." When she stood in front of him, he took her hand and pulled her onto his lap, urging her to straddle his hips, putting a knee on either side. She felt horribly exposed and vulnerable. She still had on her skirt, which now rode up extremely high. And, of course, she wasn't wearing panties. Fine time to remember that. "Rycks loves you. He's your protector. I think the situation got away from him more quickly than he realized, and it was too late to pull you back. Trust me when I tell you he's beating himself up over it now." His rough palms slid up and down her thighs in an almost mesmerizing way. "Don't ever think you're not more important than any member of his club, not to mention some hard-ass from another club. If it came to you or me, he'd slit my throat before he let anyone even form the thought of hurting you."

"Black Reign… El Diablo. El Segador. Rycks. They're not like other clubs. They've been together for a long time. Rycks and El Segador would do anything El Diablo told them to. If that meant sacrificing me, they would. I don't think he would ever do that, but who knows with El Diablo?"

"I wish I could reassure you, princess, but I don't trust any of 'em. Even Rycks. The only thing I feel I know for sure about him is that he cares for you. I believe he'd protect you with his life. It's why he allowed me in here. He knows I can free him up to find out if anyone is hunting you and who it is without having to worry he's leaving you open to attack. Did you notice in the diner he asked you if you felt safe with me?"

"Yes."

"And when you said you did, he tabled any other objections he knew you had?"

"I did."

"He'll put your safety above your comfort in any situation. He knows I'm the best man for the job and I've made a commitment to protecting you. Don't know about El Diablo or how closely Rycks obeys him, but Rycks won't hurt you or allow you to be hurt if he can prevent it."

She sighed heavily, knowing she needed to move off him but not wanting to.

"Now," he said, pulling her closer. "Let's talk about the other thing bothering you. You didn't take the morning-after pill, did you." It wasn't a question.

Mae ducked her head and shook it slightly. Now that it had all passed and she had time to think about it, she was slightly ashamed. Not in her choice -- she still had time if she changed her mind -- but that she hadn't included him in the decision.

"Want to tell me why?"

"Not really."

"Mae." He didn't sound stern or upset, just trying to make her to the right thing.

"Look, it just wasn't for me. I mean, I'm not

opposed or anything, but if I'm pregnant, I have a good support system of people who love me and who will help me if I need it. Don't get me wrong; I don't want to be pregnant, but if I am, I'll deal. It's my choice."

Then he shocked her. "Agreed. It's your body. Your choice. But if you think for a hot minute I'm gonna abandon my kid, you're dead wrong. I'd never leave my kid or his mother to fend for themselves. You've got me solidly in your corner."

Her gaze snapped to his. "Justice, I don't expect anything from you. If you want to be involved, I'm all for that. But I'm not looking for any kind of... I don't know. Commitment? Money? Anything. I've got a few hours to make up my mind, but I don't think I'm changing it."

Justice scrubbed one hand over his face while the other rested at the top of her thigh. He actually looked vulnerable. A little. Not much, but there was something there. "Princess, I'm sorry about how I acted earlier. All of it. Well, not the sex part. I'm not takin' all the blame for that. You had me with that skirt that barely stretched over your ass and that blouse with those buttons straining to contain your tits. When I saw you standing there in your underwear, there was no way I wasn't fuckin' you. I just lost my Goddamned mind."

"It wasn't all your fault, Justice," she said quietly. "I wanted to have sex with you, or I wouldn't have undressed."

* * *

For long moments they sat there. Justice sat sprawled on the couch with Mae straddling his lap. His hands molded those long, creamy thighs. He could barely glimpse the light pink flesh of her pussy. Her mound was bare and just begging for someone's tongue to lavish it with attention. He wanted that someone to be him. Fuck, just thinking about it was making his mouth water.

On impulse, he slid his hands higher to her waist and pulled her close to him. She didn't resist, but she didn't welcome him either. Instead, she looked wary.

"Is this where we do something stupid, then you start being mean to me again?"

He groaned, pulling her even closer so her forehead rested against his. "That's not goin' away anytime soon, is it?"

She shrugged. "Can't help it, Justice."

"That was a jackass move on my part," he said. "I swear to you, I'll never do it again. My only excuse is that something felt off about you. I felt like there was something I was missing and couldn't think through the haze of fuckin' lust. All I could focus on was gettin' inside your little pussy."

She shivered but maintained the conversation. "Well, you *were* missing something. Probably that I was Lucy's sister. If you knew that, you probably knew I was also living with Black Reign, and that Rycks was my guardian. All that is a pretty big deal, I suppose."

"Yeah. I guess I was also pissed at myself for not realizing how much danger you'd be in. I knew those fuckers at the DA were on the take, but I had no idea how deep the corruption was or how high up the chain it went. We all knew some, but you were the one to uncover it all. I was just so consumed with club business, even from prison, I didn't take time to figure the rest out."

"Why is that?" she asked, sitting up. "Why not appeal your conviction? I mean, I realize you were protecting the club, but you could have gotten anyone to do the work I did. I'm not a lawyer or a PI, yet I found direct links to all of them. I found the cops who actually killed the man they accused you of killing and proved how they'd set you -- and the club -- up to take the fall."

"Tell me again why you're not a lawyer?"

She blushed becomingly. "I'm not good at tests. I'm… something. Dyslexic? I see things backward sometimes. It makes it hard to read sometimes. Taking tests is an absolute nightmare. I barely passed my driver's test. Took me three tries to get my motorcycle license. So, I can't get in to law school. I barely got my GED. If it hadn't been for Rycks…"

"I get it," Justice said. "Not everyone is cut out for school. But you could definitely be a great asset for your club. I hope Rycks knows that."

"He does. He has me help on a lot of things. When I started looking into your case, he gave me free rein to do as I wanted to. I think he had Shotgun looking over my shoulder, but intel isn't his forte. He'd prefer to shoot something." She grinned, obviously trying to lighten the mood. "By the time I figured out what was happening, it was too late for Rycks to pull me back. He just told me to be careful and to not be around you. I wasn't supposed to be in court. Rycks told me he had a bad feeling about the whole thing. I guess the day I presented your case was about when he put the rest of it together. How deep everyone in the DA's office was in. By that time, it was too late. I had to continue with my part, or they'd know something was up."

"But you were still forbidden from being in court when they told me of my release."

"I wasn't letting them put you back in prison for any reason. That would put you up against every single one of their men on the inside of that place. Had you gone back for anything, they'd have torn you limb from limb."

"I'd have been all right," he said, giving her a small grin as he brushed a stay curl from her cheek behind her ear. "It wouldn't have been the first time they'd tried to get rid of me."

"Well…" She picked at a thread on the neck of his T-shirt. "I didn't want it to be the last time."

"I want to kiss you, Mae," he said, gruffly. "Then I want to take my time and taste that little pussy of yours like I should have done the first time. Will you let me?"

* * *

Because of the aftermath of the last time she'd let Justice have her, Mae swore to herself she wasn't putting herself through this again. The fact was, she wanted his touch. She wanted sex with him any way she could get it. He'd made her some promises, and she had to decide if she was willing to test them. She wasn't, but, again, she lost the battle with the part of her he called to.

When his lips claimed hers again, she just let go and resigned herself to experiencing all she could with him. If it all fell apart again, she'd tell Rycks she no longer felt safe with Justice and he'd take care of it. End of story.

Just like the last time, she was overwhelmed almost immediately. He fisted his hand in her hair and moved her where he wanted her. His tongue swept her mouth, flicking her tongue and encouraging her to play with him, too. Playful turned to nearly devastating, and Mae just rolled with it. She let him lead her down a sensual path she had no hope of escaping, even if she'd wanted to.

Somehow, she found herself being settled on her back on the couch. Justice shoved her skirt over her hips and settled his shoulders between her thighs. His beard tickled her inner thighs and the flesh of her mound. It was an erotic tickle and made her whole body clench in reaction. She couldn't decide if she wanted to pull him closer or get away from him.

She must have cried out at some point because Justice clamped a hand over her mouth. It wasn't hard or anything, just enough to make her aware he wanted her to tone it down.

"Sorry," she mumbled behind his hand.

"Don't want someone bustin' in here thinkin' I'm hurtin' you. Liable to get more of what Rycks dished out earlier, and I'm sore enough as it is."

She wanted to giggle but wasn't sure how serious he was. "I'm sorry about that," she managed, though it was hard to hold a normal conversation with his mouth between her legs and her clit on fire from his tongue, lips, and beard.

"Not your fault. Deserve what he gave me and more." Then he covered her pussy with his open mouth and groaned as he sucked. "Holy…" *Slurp.* "Fuck!" *Slurp, suck.* "So fuckin' sweet…" His tongue probed her opening deeply, which made her clit scrape across his upper lip with every move she made. Before long, Mae couldn't help her cries, and Justice must have been past caring because he used both hands to hold her hips steady.

"Oh, God!" She cried out, her hands above her head clenching the fabric of the armrest of the overstuffed couch. "Don't stop! Please, don't stop!"

He growled and inserted two fingers inside her, brushing her clit with his thumb even as he still tongued her. Higher and higher she climbed. She looked down at him, that brutally handsome face happily lapping and sucking up every drop of honey she spilled for him. Was there ever a finer sight? He was loving every second of what he was doing. No man could fake that. The longer he kept at it, the more intense he got. Groans and growls filled the air along with her cries and squeals. Every single second drove her closer to that edge of bliss he seemed determined to take her to.

Finally, she went limp, letting him take her where he wanted. The second she did, he grunted and set in with brutal intensity. As if he could have gotten any more intense. But he did. He slid his arms under her ass and lifted her to him more fully. The second he did, she fell over into oblivion.

Mae screamed, fisting her hands in his hair and grinding her pussy against his face. Justice swatted her ass once, then again. She had no idea if it was meant for her to keep still or to praise her for her responses to him, but he didn't do or say anything to make her stop so she didn't try to control herself. She just took that release and rode it until her vision blurred and she was dizzy with the pleasure of it.

He didn't let her go down easily either. Justice lifted her off the couch, urging her legs around his waist as he carried her to the bedroom. He put her on the bed and stripped off the shirt he'd given her.

"Lose the fuckin' bra," he growled. She did as he hurriedly stripped out of his clothes. By the time he stood there, fisting that magnificent cock of his, Mae was on the verge of coming again. In the back of her mind, she remembered the condom issue, but wasn't about to say anything. It wasn't that she thought he might get mad. She was actually thinking she didn't want him any way but in the raw. She wanted skin to skin. Wanted him to possess her completely and to possess him. While she wasn't sure about his commitment to her, she believed him when he said he'd make sure she was taken care of. He knew the score. If he didn't want a tie to her, he knew what to do. So she waited to see what would happen.

Chapter Four

Justice was being a bastard yet again. No way he was using a condom. No way he was letting this woman out of his sight for the foreseeable future. Did he want her pregnant? If anyone had asked him that the second he'd met her, Justice would have scoffed, but might not have said an outright "no." When he realized what he'd done when they'd fucked earlier, he might have given a "hell, no" response, but he wasn't sure he'd have meant it wholeheartedly. Now? He wasn't sure. The thought of a little baby bump in his line of sight as he looked up into her eyes while devouring her had some appeal he was afraid to examine too closely.

As he lowered himself on top of Mae, he looked intently at her face. She had a look of a woman in a lust-induced lethargy, but she reached for him eagerly.

"Justice," she whispered.

"Archer." No one called him that. But he wanted Mae to.

She got an adorably confused look on her face. "I -- what?"

"My name," he said patiently, settling himself at her entrance. "If we're gonna continue this, you need to get used to callin' me by my name."

"Archer," she said, her brow furrowing as if thinking about what he'd said. "Archer." She met his gaze again. "I knew that. Sounds much better hearing you say it, though. Also, I think it fits you. I guess I've always thought of bikers in terms of their street names. I've always thought of you as Justice." Her eyes were wide, and a beautiful shade of dark blue he could look at for days. There was uncertainty there, but a hope that made his heart ache. She wasn't a woman who gave herself to just anyone. She hadn't been a virgin, but he'd bet she could count on one hand the number of lovers she'd had. And he was asking her for everything. "I-I need to know why you want me to call you that."

"No one else does. Not my brothers. Not my family. Even my mother calls me Justice."

Her gaze cleared, but he could feel her little pussy winking at him where his dick was resting just at the entrance. "Does she know why you let yourself get sent to prison?"

"She does." It was a sore subject between him and his mother. His father had understood, but his mother just wanted her son.

"And she was OK with it?"

"Not at all, Mae. But she understood. It was why she started calling me Justice when she found out that was my road name. She said it suited me."

"So, why do you want me to call you Archer?"

"Because you're different from anyone else in my life. And because you're mine. There should be something special between us that no one else shares."

"You don't love me," she said, shaking her head. "I don't love you."

Surprisingly, Justice felt a pang when she said she didn't love him. Did he want her love? Maybe he did. "I know, princess. It may come in time. May not. For either of us. But I want to see where this goes."

"I don't share," she said without flinching. "You want to be with me for now, fine. But I won't have you bed-hopping on me. I can't do that."

He flashed her a lopsided smile as he flexed his hips and eased inside her. Her eyes widened and she sucked in a little gasp. "While we're together, neither of us takes another lover. We can agree on that."

Mae nodded her head eagerly. "Yes. Yes!"

"Good." Then Justice started to move slowly inside her. The wet heat of her pussy made him need to come as soon as possible. Nothing could ever feel this good. He'd certainly never known anything like sex with Mae existed. He'd thought the first time had been a fluke, but this had been even better. He wanted to blame it on prison, but it wasn't that. And he damned sure didn't want to come. Not yet.

Mae clung to him so sweetly, digging her little nails into his back. Her heels dug into his ass and lower back while she tilted her pelvis, meeting him thrust for thrust. The closer she got to coming, the more she clawed at Justice.

"I… Archer! Oh, God!"

"That's it, princess. You need this?"

"Yes." It came out a little whimper. Justice found her mouth and kissed it just because he thought she needed it.

Sure enough, she met each thrust of his tongue with one of her own. It made his cock twitch, which made her pussy ripple, which made that need to come so much sharper. He needed to stop a moment, to find his bearings. Mae was having none of that. She nipped his lip, and all Justice could do was readjust his position, wrap his arms more securely around her, and fuck the shit out of her.

Mae screamed before biting down on his shoulder. That little bit of pain was all Justice could stand. "You come with me, Mae! Fuckin' come now!"

She did. Her little pussy squeezed and milked Justice for all he was worth. Back arching, Justice gave a bellow to the ceiling before remembering somewhere in the back of his mind that being quiet was high on his list of priorities at the moment.

Keeping himself as deep as he could, Justice growled as he looked down into the fathomless blue eyes of the woman who'd wrapped herself around his insides in the space of a few hours. What the fuck was he going to do? Because, when he thought about it, letting her get away from him wasn't an option. He wasn't certain how long he wanted to keep her, but it damned sure was longer than he'd first thought. And fuck it, he hoped like fucking hell she was actually pregnant. He'd deal with Rycks when that time came, but in that moment, Justice decided he had two goals in his life.

These were in no particular order, but ideally, first thing he'd do was to make sure anyone thinking to come after Mae met with a gruesome end. No matter the cost to him. Second, he was going to knock Mae up. Get her pregnant with his kid as soon as possible. After that, he'd figure out how to keep her happy so she stayed with him. Because, yeah. He wasn't even ready to admit it to himself, but he wasn't ever letting Mae go. Mae Stephens… was his.

* * *

The next two weeks were pretty dull. Well, except for the sex. Mae walked around with a smile on her face everywhere she went. Also, true to his word, Justice was never far from her side. Though there still seemed to be some concern as to her and Justice's safety, nothing had happened. She knew she'd be a fool to believe it had all gone away. It had only been two weeks. But no one had made a move to harm her, and there had been no threats or messages delivered to Black Reign or Salvation's Bane. Mae was hoping Rycks and Justice were wrong, and she wasn't in as much of a pickle as they'd first thought.

Staying in the compound wasn't a hardship

when she had Justice to keep her company, but she knew he wanted to get out and about in the city. After being in prison for eight years, who wouldn't? He was also getting a bit grouchy. It was the only thing truly marring her happiness because she was sure he was starting to regret the whole not-using-a-condom thing. Because, yeah. They'd had sex every single day -- sometimes several times a day -- for two solid weeks.

"Come on," she said, taking his hand. They'd been sitting by the pool in the back of the compound. Now, she pointed toward the garage. "We're going on a ride."

He shook his head, but he stood when she tugged at him. "Not a good idea. Ain't found anyone keepin' an eye on the place, but that don't mean they ain't."

"Rycks has called in Bones to help. If Data and Suzie can't find anything, I doubt there's anything to worry about."

"Ain't really the outside I'm worryin' about."

She tilted her head. "Here or Bane?"

"Bane. Black Reign didn't have El Diablo as the head when I went to prison. Someone inside Bane helped kill that motherfucker I took the hit for. When the DA turned to Salvation's Bane in that investigation, he should have come forward to the club, or at least brought it to Thorn, but he didn't." He shrugged. "At least, that's my theory. Ain't got no proof, but their evidence wasn't fabricated that time and it all pointed to a messy kill by Bane. Which means someone on the inside."

"Or just a messy kill. Or someone setting you up. Or any number of things," Mae protested. "You don't know it was from inside the club."

"No," Justice agreed as he followed her to the

garage. "Just a feelin'." He seemed to get distracted as he looked at his bike longingly. Yeah. The man needed to ride.

Mae snagged her helmet, knowing there was no way he'd let her ride her own bike. "Come on, Archer," she said. His name had gotten easier for her to remember to use, though Justice suited him better. The second she'd said it, his gaze snapped to her and the heat radiating from it nearly made her rethink her plan to make him ride. "Nope. Maybe later. You're getting PMS" -- parked motorcycle syndrome --"and I'm tired of hearing the rest of the club bitch about it."

His head snapped back as if she'd slapped him, a shocked look on his face. "I've not been bitchy."

"No. But you've been moody. And you growl at anyone getting close to me. Also, I heard one of the club girls telling the others this afternoon that if I couldn't take care of you, they were going to have to. Since I've been doing my level best to catch you up on fucking from your long stint in the big house -- and I feel like I'm doing all I can do there and you're still grouchy -- I racked my brain to think of something I'd forgotten. Since I can't allow the girls to corrupt you without a killing, which is what got you in trouble in the first damned place, I had to think outside the box."

"And PMS is what you came up with." He scowled at her, but she could see his lips twitch.

"Tell me I'm wrong and I'll apologize."

"Smart ass." He got on his bike and started it up, revving it several times before backing it out of the garage. "Hop on, princess."

She did, eagerly, not too ashamed to admit she'd missed riding too. As they sat in the driveway preparing to take off, she saw Rycks on the porch. She threw up a hand at him and he nodded. Mae knew he didn't want her away from the safety of the clubhouse, yet he was willing to let her go with Justice. To her, that said a lot about his trust in her protector. As she knew he would, Justice noticed Rycks, too. He gave Rycks a two-fingered salute, then they were on their way.

Mae lifted her face to the warm afternoon sun and laughed. This was absolutely what she needed. In one of the mirrors on the bike, she noticed Justice quirking a smile as they sped down the highway. Yeah. They both needed this.

They rode for a long, long time. Not stopping, not talking. Justice just kept them steady on the road at a leisurely pace while Mae enjoyed the scenery. From time to time, he'd tap her knee and point to something he thought she'd like to see. It was as if they'd been together for years instead of a couple of weeks. With the wind whirling around them, Justice's scent surrounded her. Sometimes, she put her face against his back or at his neck and just inhaled. Somewhere deep inside her, she was certain she wanted this for the rest of her life.

As they continued down the road, Mae noticed Justice didn't seem as relaxed as he had been at the start. He continually looked around them, glancing in the mirrors several times. Instead of making his way to the first interstate entrance, he went off the highway, deeper into the wilds. It wasn't long before the paved road gave way to a narrow, dirt strip. If she was right, they were on the south west side of Lake Okeechobee, in the wooded areas. Justice must have known exactly where he was going because they didn't run into swamp land on the bike, which would have surely gotten them stuck beyond getting out on their own.

Finally, he stopped on a small knoll edged in

thick trees with swamp and marshes beyond. It had to be the one place in the whole area he could maneuver that bike and not have it get swallowed by the swamp.

When he turned off the bike, Justice gripped her knee. A warning to stay still. A moment later, she heard it. Some kind of vehicle off in the distance. It was hard to say how far away, but considering the winding road -- if you could call it that -- and no other path to follow, it was a safe bet they were being followed.

"Get behind that tree," he said, indicating a big cypress tree close by but far enough away she'd be hidden. He tossed her his cell. "Things go south, you get as far away as quietly as you can. That phone has satellite service, so once you know you've not got someone on your ass, call Rycks."

"What's going on?" Mae was starting to panic now. Why had he taken them so deep into the wilderness?

"Gettin' ready to have company. You have that knife with you?"

"The one I got busted with at the courthouse? Yeah. You told me to always keep it with me."

"Good. If they get by me, can you kill anyone who comes at you?" She nodded silently. "Then be ready. Likely won't be a need, and I'd rather you run. You're lighter and faster than most men. If it comes to it, though, don't hesitate."

He turned away from her, not waiting for a response. Mae's heart raced. He could have gone back to the clubhouse. Either of them. Did he not want her around his club? Was she too much of a liability? Then why not take her back to Black Reign?

Was she the bait for a trap he'd set?

That was stupid. She was the one who'd dragged him to the bike. But he'd set the course. And hadn't he texted someone just before they left? Rycks had been there looking on. Did he know about this? Maybe she should call him now.

Yes. That's what she should do. She punched in Rycks's number and waited for it to ring. Instead of answering, however, her call went to voicemail.

"We're in trouble," she said as calmly as she could. That would be enough. If she said more and anyone intercepted the message, she could be signing their death warrants. She also fired off a text. Nothing. She was about to yell out her frustration when the vehicle -- a Jeep of some kind -- pulled up a distance from Justice's bike and stopped. Three big bruisers got out. Two of them had long, thick batons of some kind. The other had a gun, but it remained in a shoulder holster under his left arm. Mae crouched behind the tree and kept as still as she could and still keep Justice and the three men in sight.

"Where's the girl?" one of them said. His voice was rough in a menacing way. There was almost a sneer to it, as if he were going to take pleasure in whatever was about to happen next.

"Gone." Justice's reply was clipped. He stood still, his arms loose at his sides. Mae could tell by his posture and the wildness on his face he was readying himself for battle.

"Make it easy for us to find her and we'll kill you quickly. Otherwise, it's gonna be a long day." The same guy grinned, looking around them as if to indicate his point. "Ain't no one around to hear your screams."

"Or to find your bodies," Justice countered.

In a move so fast Mae almost missed it, the guy with the gun drew his weapon and fired. Justice was already on the ground when the other guys charged him. At first Mae thought he was hit and had to hold back a cry by biting on the fingers of one hand. In her other, she gripped the hilt of the knife in a tight fist, the blade resting lightly on her forearm like Rycks had taught her. Vaguely she knew she needed to get the little can of pepper spray out of her pocket and ready for quick use, but she was too terrified for Justice to put her thoughts into action.

Mae knew Justice had a gun, but he didn't pull it. Instead, he rolled to his feet, meeting his attackers head on as one with batons charged for him. He ducked under the first one, neatly taking the guy's weapon. Using the forward momentum he'd gained, Justice slammed baton into the second guy's head with skull-shattering force. The guy with the gun got off another shot but again, missed his target. By that time Justice was on him, smashing the baton down on the guy's gun arm, then back up to his head in a glancing blow. His second swing came just as the last guy reached Justice. He managed to land another blow to the gunman's head, though not as devastating as before, just as the third guy swung. Justice ducked, barely missing getting his head bashed in. The gunman wasn't so lucky. His partner hit him full in the face. Blood spurted everywhere as the gunman went down. When Justice rose, he hit the guy. With a brutal yell, Justice brought the baton sideways across his body to in the side of his head. Again, blood sprayed in a wide arc from where the wooden bat impacted.

Mae was breathing harder than Justice. The man looked as if he'd barely broken a sweat. He'd certainly dispatched three enemies with brutal efficiency. As afraid as she was, Mae was awed at his speed, strength, and the purposeful way he fought. There was no hesitation whatsoever. He'd simply done what he had to do. In her heart, Mae knew those men were dead, or, at least, would be before they left the swamp. She didn't blame Justice. In a way, it just cemented why he was called Justice. To her, it wasn't because he used to be a lawyer. He brought justice where the law couldn't.

"Mae!" he called. "You good?"

She stepped out from her hiding place. "I'm good," she managed, though her voice wavered.

"Stay on this side of the tree where I can see you unless I say otherwise."

She nodded again. "I need to call Rycks. I tried, but only got voicemail."

"No need, princess. He knows. If he don't, he will soon." He turned back to the scene of carnage.

"What are you doing?" she called, moving toward him.

"Cleaning up. No!" he snapped when she turned to see her headed his way. "Stay there. I'll come get you when I'm done."

"I can help --"

"No, Mae." He practically growled at her. "I need you as far from this scene as I can get you and still keep an eye on you. My brothers will be here soon to help. Rycks will be here for you. Just wait there. Keep your eyes and ears open. You'll be my lookout."

"Like you need a lookout," she muttered before yelling at him in her fear and frustration, "What's going on?"

Justice turned back to her, annoyance on his face. "Let me finish this. When I come home, we'll talk."

"Fine. Let me tell you what I think is going on." Mae pointed an accusing finger at him even as she fought back tears. "You used me as bait! You took me on a ride to draw them out. You knew they wouldn't attack the club so you got me away from it."

"Mae, can we not do this now?"

"We don't have to do anything. Just do whatever you have to do so we can get out of here."

Justice didn't answer her, just turned back to the carnage and started working. He put all three men in the car, then got in himself. He moved it to the edge of the swamp, next to another big, gnarled cypress. The tree had fallen long ago and was propped by a neighboring tree. There was no way it was falling any time soon, but the roots had been pulled from the wet, muddy soil, leaving a large swath of displaced mud and vegetation. Immediately, the car sank with its weight.

The front was almost sunk past the top of the doors before Justice even started to climb out. Though the car seemed to have stopped sinking, Mae still let go a scream of denial.

"NO! Justice!"

He stumbled free, looking around him as if expecting something to be there for him. When nothing happened, he turned back to her, pointing an accusing finger at her.

"I told you to fuckin' call me Archer." Justice stalked toward her, a look equal parts annoyance and lust on his handsome face. Everything about this man called to her. Had from the moment she'd seen him in that courthouse. She didn't want to think he'd betrayed her, that he'd chosen to keep his club safe at risk to her. He wasn't offering an alternative theory, but she was still drawn to him like a moth to a flame.

"I'm not calling you anything but asshole! Or maybe rat bastard!" He stalked closer and Mae took an involuntary step backward. When she did, a big hand landed on her shoulder. She yelped and jerked away, moving toward Justice for protection.

"It's all right, Mae. You're safe." Rycks stood there in the clearing with her and Justice, his hand on her shoulder. "I'm sorry I scared you, honey. I just came to make sure you and Justice were good. Salvation's Bane has a couple more men coming to help Justice secure this scene so no one ever finds these guys."

"At least, not until the gators have had their fill of 'em." Justice wiped his forearm over his brow and winced when he did. For the first time, she noticed him favoring his left side. He moved to put an arm around her, but Mae stepped sideways and he groaned. "Fuck, Mae. Just… fuck." Scrubbing a hand through his hair, he actually winced this time. "It's nothing like what you're thinking. This was a purely instinctive move on my part. It wasn't planned ahead of time, but the boys were ready because they've been tracking both of us since we realized how much trouble there was."

"He's telling the truth," Rycks said softly.

"You!" She whirled on him, stabbing a finger against his chest. "You're just as guilty as he is! You all planned this! With me in the middle!" She was so angry and hurt and scared now she had no hope of holding back the tears. A sob escaped her. "Why? Why would you do that?"

"Princess, calm the fuck down." Justice's tone wasn't as sharp as his words. He kept looking around them, searching for something. As soon as two more men came into view, coming through the swamp, he relaxed visibly. "Come with me. We'll sort this out at the clubhouse."

"I'm not going anywhere with you!" She glanced at Rycks. "Either of you!"

"You gotta go with someone, honey. You can't walk."

"Fine. Just get me to the road. I'll call my sister and get the fuck out of here."

"Good. Get on the bike."

"Guys, you need to go. Now." One of the men who'd just showed up approached them. "El Segador says the DA's office is requesting to meet with Mae. They want her in their office this afternoon."

"Tell them they can go through her lawyer," Rycks said. "She's not doing anything tonight but talking to me and Justice."

"I'll go where I want to go," she protested.

"Honey, you know the DA's office is dirty. These men were likely sent by them. They probably think their men have already killed you and are trying to put the club on notice. They'll get us looking for you, then make their move on Justice. At least, that's what they're thinking they'll do. They don't know their men are dead yet."

"And when they figure it out," Justice added, "they're gonna know you know what happened to them and they're gonna come after you and me both."

"But not the club," she spat. "You two managed to keep both Salvation's Bane and Black Reign safe. Just not me."

"For fuck's sake," Justice said, lunging for her and grabbing her arm. "Get on the fuckin' bike and let's get the fuck outa here." He actually picked her up and set her on the back of his bike, thrusting the helmet on her head before climbing on himself. Rycks followed them and stood by her side.

"I swear you've got it wrong, little flower," he said. Mae wanted to deny him, but he looked so stricken she thought she might believe him. It would seem out of character considering her experience with him. He'd always been about protecting her and

Serilda and Winter. Why would he suddenly change? Maybe it was all Justice.

"I just want to go home," she whimpered, knowing she was about to lose her shit in a huge way.

"Then go with Justice. He'll take you home, and I'll meet you there after we've finished up here."

She turned away, unable to look at him any longer. If she did, she'd forgive him. If she forgave him, she'd have to forgive Justice, and she wasn't ready to do that. Justice started up the big Harley, giving a nod to Rycks before he did. Then they were off.

The ground was rougher on the way out than she remembered going in. Probably because she was hyper aware of everything around her now, expecting someone to jump out at them or to hear a gunshot over the roar of the Harley's pipes.

When they reached the pavement, Justice sped up. He went faster still when they reached the highway and didn't let up until they pulled into the Black Reign compound. With the gates securely locked behind them, Justice pulled his bike around the back, not stopping to let Mae off until he'd parked where he intended to stay put.

"Come on," he said, as he climbed off, dragging her with him.

"Let me go," she said, but her heart wasn't in it. Deep down, she wanted him to convince her he hadn't put her at risk to save the fucking club. That was something she'd often heard about in other clubs but had never seen it herself in Black Reign. All these years, she'd convinced herself they were different. That Salvation's Bane was different. Now, she wasn't sure, and it was breaking her heart.

Chapter Five

Justice knew he'd fucked up. Like big time. Just not for the reason Mae thought. Getting her back to the room they shared was going to take some doing.

"I told you to let me go, asshole!" She pulled on his hold, twisting her hand to get out of his grip. When they entered the common room, several of the club members sat up straighter or stood, tensing. Ready to come to her defense.

"No," he growled, adjusting his hold so he was higher up on her arm. The last thing he wanted to do was to bruise her tender skin. Not this way. Any marks like that on her body would come from fierce lovemaking, not her struggling to get away from him. "Stop squirmin'!"

A few of the guys approached them, surrounding them when Mae showed no sign of letting up. "There a problem?" Samson, one of the biggest fuckers Justice had ever seen, looked from him to Mae, standing squarely in Justice's path.

"No," Justice said at the same time Mae yelled, "Yes!"

"OK, maybe we need to take a break," Samson said, his face hard. Though he was still calm, it was easy to tell the man was beyond irritated. They all knew Justice had basically claimed Mae. He hadn't put a property patch on her yet -- it was way too soon for that. Besides, if he decided that was his next move with her, he'd do it at his own fuckin' clubhouse. "Put her down, Justice."

"She's my woman. You tellin' me you're comin' between us? 'Cause I'll take that shit very fuckin' personal." OK, so maybe that was a little heavy, but he was beginning to panic. Something he'd never felt in his life.

"She belongs to Black Reign, Justice. You ain't claimed her. Until that happens, she's ours to protect."

Justice bared his teeth, aware he was probably going to have to fight the man, and that he couldn't kill him. Samson probably didn't have the same compunction about killing Justice.

"All right, all right." The clipped, slightly British accent carried across the room as El Diablo stepped out onto the landing above them, immediately followed by two women. They stood on either side of the man, one gripping his arm, the other rubbing her face against his arm. Both were tall, leggy, and busty, wearing... not much at all. "Mae, my dear. Is there a problem?"

Justice tensed. If Mae insisted he let her go, El Diablo would most definitely force the issue.

"Just have him let me go and I'm good."

Justice looked at Mae and shook his head. "Ain't happenin', princess. We got things to discuss."

"If the lady doesn't want to talk to you, she doesn't have to," El Diablo said, but gave no further order. "Perhaps if you tell me what the problem is we can help you work it out."

Mae held Justice's gaze. He could see her uncertainty. If she voiced what she had to him before, she risked alienating El Diablo. So it came down to how much she trusted him. And if she didn't fully trust Rycks...

Finally, she sighed. "He wants to try to convince me that he and Rycks didn't just set me up as bait to catch some of the people threatening me. We were followed and attacked by three guys, and he knew he had no one to help him fight."

El Diablo cocked his head, looking for all the world as if he didn't understand what she'd just said.

"Bait?"

"They were trying to ambush us," Justice said softly. "Instead of going straight to the Salvation's Bane clubhouse, or back here, I led them to a remote section of swamp so we could take care of them. She believes it was done intentionally."

"It had to have been!" Mae looked at him accusingly before returning her attention to El Diablo. "You didn't tell anyone where we were going because we didn't know when we left! You knew there'd be someone chasing me, and you drove around until they spotted us, then you took them out so you could... so they'd be..."

Mae's face nearly crumbled. Two tears left her eyes in rapid succession before she took a deep breath. She was still in shock from the violence. Justice knew there had been some problems when she and Lucrecia had first come on their scene. That was not long after he went to prison. Was she remembering some violence done to her then?

El Diablo looked impassive, as if none of this affected him in any way. The two women with El Diablo had draped themselves artfully over him on either side. Despite them rubbing themselves against him, their tits barely concealed by black leather bras and bustiers, El Diablo ignored them completely. One wore leather boy shorts, the other a leather thong. Both wore black strappy heels. El Diablo didn't seem to realize they were even there for all the attention he paid them. "If you didn't deliberately set up the situation," he said with a dismissive wave to Justice, "how did Rycks and your men know to meet you there?"

"We set up tracking devices on both me and Mae, as well as both our bikes. It's two-way, so I can send out a signal for help. While I had no intention of being anywhere without her, there was always the possibility she'd sneak off on her own, and I hadn't told her about it yet. We just got them installed a few days ago. I needed to make sure everyone could locate us if it became necessary."

"I see." El Diablo smiled, not unkindly, but Justice noticed the smile didn't quite reach his eyes. "Unfortunately, you didn't answer the question."

"When I knew we were being followed, I activated the locator on my bike. I couldn't take them to Bane because Lucrecia is pregnant. I couldn't bring them back here because they were between us and the clubhouse, and I didn't have eyes on them. There was every possibility they weren't alone. Taking them deep into the wilds next to Lake Okeechobee was my first instinct. Get them away from prying eyes and get rid of them."

"Not sure I'm following," El Diablo said in an unctuous tone, not sounding as though he cared one way or the other and making it perfectly clear what he thought of Justice's intellect. "Surely someone with your knowledge of, shall we say, physical combat, should know three against one are not flattering odds. Even worse, you had no idea how many people were actually following you. Am I right?"

There was an uncomfortable silence. Justice did not want to answer that question. He didn't want to explain the true reason he took that lot to the swamp. Mae would never accept what he'd done, but really, it was the only thing he could do.

Finally, he sighed, turning to Mae. "I did what I did because it gave me the best chance of keeping you safe."

"I'm afraid you're going to have to explain," El

Diablo said, moving around the women at his side and down the stairs to face Justice. "Little Mae deserves to be more than just a means to exact revenge for your little eight-year vacation."

And that was really the heart of it, wasn't it? If Justice had to say in the moment whether or not he'd killed those men to keep Mae safe or avenge himself, he wasn't sure what his answer would be.

Then he turned to Mae. There was a confused look on her face, as if she wasn't sure what El Diablo was getting at. When she looked back to Justice, he knew.

"I'm not a good man, Mae," Justice said, holding her gaze. "I've dreamed about revenge for eight fuckin' years. Maybe some part of me did want revenge on those fuckers, but I want you to really hear what I'm getting ready to tell you. It's going to scare you, and you're probably going to want to leave me, but you need to know." Her eyes went wide, like a child about to learn who Santa Claus really was and not sure she really wanted to know. She nodded at him to continue. Justice had an overwhelming urge to pull her into his arms. What if this was the last time he got to hold her?

When he pulled her into his arms, she didn't resist. She even hugged him back. The feel of her little fingers curling into his shirt gave him the courage he needed to admit what he'd done.

"I took us to that place instead of one of the clubhouses because it was the only way I could guarantee I could protect you."

She shook her head. "You were one man alone."

"I was one man willing to do anything to protect you. Until El Diablo asked me my motives, I can honestly say getting revenge for them railroading me into prison never crossed my mind. Even if it did, those guys weren't the ones who put me there."

"If not revenge, then what?" Mae looked to be on the verge of tears, but she was holding herself together. Giving him the chance to come clean. Did he dare? The only thing he knew for sure was, if he didn't, she'd never trust him again. Hell, it would probably shake her faith in Rycks and what was essentially her club. Salvation's Bane, his club, was the only thing that got him through prison. If he'd lost faith in his club, there was no way he'd have made it eight years in that hell hole. He couldn't let her lose faith. Not like that. It was the only thing that gave him the courage to tell her.

"I'm a killer, Mae. You freed a killer from prison." She shook her head, but he continued. "I took us to that remote place because there was no way I was lettin' you get hurt. If I took you to either clubhouse, I had to be careful about what I did. It's not like either clubhouse is in the middle of town, but they're not remote enough to kill and have no one notice." He sighed. "I took you there because I never intended those men to live. Out there, I didn't have to be careful. I could do whatever I had to."

No one said anything for long moments. When Mae finally spoke, her voice was quiet. Rough. "You intended to kill them to keep me safe? Why not just… I don't know. Wound them?"

"Because they might come back."

She blinked up at him several times. Was the truth of what he'd done impacting her? Would she reject him?

"Sounds like he doesn't take chances with your life, little Mae." El Diablo was quiet and non-threatening as he stood in front of Mae. He laid a hand on her shoulder and his whole demeanor changed. The look he gave her was one of gentle affection. "Don't be too quick to judge. His heart --"

"Is good," Mae finished in a whisper. "He's a good man."

"That he is. Loyal to a fault. He gave up eight years of his life for his club and was willing to do it again for you. Only this time, he was willing to not only take the fall, but do the crime as well." He looked Justice up and down, assessing him. "Little rough around the edges, but you could do worse. Besides. Not only was he thinking about you, but he considered your sister and her unborn child. Remember that as well, little Mae."

Mae launched herself at Justice, sobbing as she did. She clung to him and Justice held her just as tightly. A knot in his chest he hadn't realized was there unraveled, and he could breathe easier.

"One more thing." Justice turned so that Mae could look at El Diablo when he spoke. "Don't be hard on Rycks over this. He has demons. Some of which compel him to care for strays like you and the sweet Winter and lovely Serilda. He would never let anyone use you as bait. No matter the reason."

"Let's go upstairs," Justice urged. "We have to talk."

"OK."

* * *

Mae's head was spinning. Why would he risk himself and going back to prison for her? "If you'd just gone back to the clubhouse, Rycks and El Diablo and everyone else could have backed you up," she muttered. "How did Rycks even know where to find us? What the fuck? Let me go, Justice!" She'd been mulling it all over on the way to her room. Once inside she needed space. Surprisingly, he let her go. But he stayed between her and the door.

"Shotgun had a line on me and you at all times. When I activated my bike's homing signal, he knew it was an emergency, especially given the area I was headed."

"He knew where you were going."

"I'd told him that, if I got in a spot where I knew I was gonna have to kill, that swamp was where I'd go. When he saw where I was headed, he knew who and what to send, including Rycks. The boys got the place cleaned up and the bodies and car disposed of. Will someone find them? Yeah. Eventually. Hopefully not for a few years. By then, the gators should have done their job."

For some reason, that last bit made her giggle. All the tension of the past couple hours gave way to a horrible bout of giggling until she was finally laughing so hard tears were rolling down her cheeks.

"Not sure I see what's funny, but I'll take it," he said, pulling her close.

"I wish I could tell you, but, honestly, I'm not sure. I think maybe the whole thing... I don't know. You're really serious about it. You really did all that just to protect me, and you make no apologies for it."

"When it comes to you? No. No apologies. I'm not willing to go to prison without a fight but only because that leaves you open to attack. I kill anyone they send after you and get arrested or convicted, they'll come after you hard because I won't be there. I ain't willin' to leave your safety to anyone else if I can help it."

"I don't want you going back to prison."

"So you understand why I did what I did? Can you live with that blood? It's not on your hands, but mine are coated with it."

"I can because those guys were evil. They were

willing to kill for money, and their employers were willing to kill an innocent person just to give you a message. They're all evil."

"Yeah, baby. They are."

Justice sat on the bed they'd shared for weeks now. When he did, he winced, his hand going to cover his left side. Mae stood in front of him and reached for his shirt.

"Get this off," she said. "You're hurt."

"Ain't nothin'. Guy just got in a lucky punch."

"Lucky punches can still knock you out. Let's have a look."

Peeling the shirt from Justice's body was a luxury in itself. He was perfectly made, and his ink enhanced his body's beauty rather than covering it up. It seemed like every tattoo was placed in such a way that it drew the eye to every ridge and hollow of the muscle it graced. He was truly a work of art.

When he raised his arms, he winced again, and Mae could see the reddish-purple bruise forming along his side. It was quite possible he had some broken ribs.

"I'm getting Rycks. You need a doctor."

"I promise I'll go see Blade tomorrow. Right now, I just want you."

"You're not really in any shape to fuck me, Justice."

"Never said I was gonna fuck you." He had a mulish look about him as he eased back on the bed, as if it didn't really matter what kind of shape he was in, he was doing what he wanted. "But I do want to make love to you and hold you. If it makes you feel better, I'll let you be on top."

"Why do I have the feeling you're setting me up?"

"No idea. But yeah. Strip off and come ride me."

"I'm not going to get you to take it easy, am I? You're not going to the doctor." She didn't bother asking. She also stripped to his avid gaze.

"Nope. Definitely not right now."

Once nude, Mae climbed onto the bed and straddled Justice. His cock poked at her entrance even before she reached behind her to guide him inside. The second she did, a greedy moan escaped her. There was no hiding how much she wanted Justice, and she didn't even try. After the pain she'd felt at what she'd thought was a betrayal, she knew there was no fighting her attraction to him. She wanted him as long as she could have him. If that was a day or a month, or a year, she'd take it. If that made her weak, then she just wasn't a strong person. The thing was, she believed Justice. She believed Rycks and El Diablo. This was her family. Justice was her love.

Giving herself up to the sensations, Mae braced her hands on his chest and rose and fell as she needed. Sometimes she'd give a little twist of her hips and he'd groan, squeezing her thighs. When he wasn't gripping her legs, Justice ran his rough, callused hands up and down her legs, then up her sides to cup her breasts. When her breath caught, he pulled her down to him until he latched onto one nipple, pulling strongly.

Mae's whole body shuddered, and she thrust her breast at him, offering more. So he found the other nipple with his mouth. This time he bit down gently. Mae's cunt squeezed around his dick when she sucked in a breath.

"More," she sighed.

Justice grunted and pulled her farther down, fisting his hand in her hair and kissing her passionately. His tongue swept into her mouth to tangle with hers as she sank down on his cock.

Finally, he wrapped his arms around her tightly, one hand on her back, the other on her ass. Then he surged up, driving his cock deeper into her grasping, weeping pussy.

Mae cried out, throwing her head back. Justice took advantage and latched on to her neck. Never had Mae felt so alive! Every single time he made love to her, Justice brought her a new and wonderful experience. His cock pulsed inside her, stretching the skin below her clit so she had just enough sensation on the sensitive bud to keep her on the edge but not to push her over. She shifted her hips a little bit and got the friction she needed.

"Gonna come!" Her cry sounded desperate even to herself as she moved faster and faster, meeting Justice's thrust with her own. Then she fell. The orgasm washed over her so hard she sobbed his name. Dimly, she knew Justice came with her, knew that he'd found just as much pleasure as she had.

Always. She wanted it to always be this good. Both of them were breathing hard. Sweat slickened their bodies as they moved against each other. If sex had a distinctive smell, Mae knew she was surrounded by it now. Musky, slightly sweet, and the combined scent of the woodsy outdoors and motor oil emanating from Justice.

He rolled them over so he lay on top of her. He thrust once, but she felt him flinch when he did. Yeah. Justice was still hurting. Probably even more than before they'd had sex.

"Let me up," she whispered, stroking his face and kissing him once more just because she needed to.

"Not a chance, princess. You ain't leavin' this bed for a long while."

"I'm not lying here and letting you fuck me

when you're obviously hurting. Now, get up and let me wash. We've had a long day. I think we both need to rest. Then you need to go see the doc. If you don't want to leave here for a while, Black Reign has a really good club doc. His name's Fury."

"Fine. But not today. I'm still hurtin' tomorrow, I'll call Blade. Ain't seein' no doc named Fury."

She giggled. "Are you scared of needles?"

"Nope. Just docs named Fury with needles."

Chapter Six

Wrath, a member of Black Reign Justice had only recently become aware of, not only put off the DA's office twenty-four hours, but had refused to let Mae meet with them for a solid week and a half. Why? "Because I fuckin' felt like it." From what Justice had been able to gather from his contacts both in and out of prison, Wrath was a world-renowned lawyer adept at not only the art of law in several different countries, but at keeping a low profile. As such, very few recognized his real name, and those who did never crossed him. In court or out of it.

So by the time Wrath led Mae to the DA's office, there was nothing about Mae and Justice he didn't know. He also demanded to know the content of the discussion they had planned for Mae and was prepared to pull her out should they deviate from that script at all. He'd practiced with Mae for hours but told her he never intended for her to say a fuckin' word. If they required an answer, she was to keep her fuckin' mouth shut unless he gave her permission. Justice wasn't allowed anywhere near the DA's office. Naturally, that hadn't gone over well with Justice or Mae, but from what Justice had learned, that was actually Wrath being nice.

"I trust this meeting will be short." Wrath, aka Vincent Black, held a chair for Mae when they entered the spacious conference room. Shotgun had hacked into the cameras recording the meeting, and Justice now watched and listened to it from the large monitor on Shotgun's desk with earphones straddling his head.

"I'm sorry. I don't believe we've met." The assistant DA stood and offered his hand. "Jamison Devo."

Wrath looked down at the offered hand and sneered. "Vincent Black. I'm Miss Stephen's lawyer." He didn't shake Devo's hand. "I'm aware of the questions you wish to pose to my client. I want it entered into the record that we came voluntarily and that, while we are cooperating, we object highly to the interview in general."

"We just wish to clear up some matters regarding the case Miss Stephens made that led to the release of the dangerous gangster, Archer 'Justice' Creed. The introduction of such… outlandish evidence, while wholly without basis, convinced a judge to not only release Mr. Creed, but to do it with prejudice. We'd like to know how she came by the so-called evidence." Justice knew then the DA's office had no idea how she'd found anything. They were hoping she'd tell them how she beat them at their own game.

"Yes, I suppose you would." Wrath rolled his eyes in exasperation, like a king to a stupid subordinate. Justice knew the show of irritation was by design, not a show of temper on Wrath's part. The man was a perfectionist and an expert at manipulation. "My suggestion would be for you to follow up on those points raised by Miss Stephens. You want to know where her evidence came from, backtrack it. Isn't that what investigators do? You've got cops out there investigating." He waved his hand in a little circle. "Have them continue. She doesn't need to tell you how she found her information. I believe any discovery she needed to pass on was done. Which is why Mr. Creed was freed in the first place."

"I understand," Devo continued. "But if we're to pursue this, to try members of our own office, we need to know everything she knows."

Wrath snorted. "We're done here, Mac." He

stood, prompting Mae to do the same. "They're fishing. You're not doing their job for them."

"We're not done." The DA, William Barrison, raised his voice angrily.

"Are you charging my client with something, Mr. Barrison? If so, I'm going to need the warrant now." When Barrison simply stuck out his chin stubbornly, Wrath smirked at him. "I thought not. We're done when I say we're done."

"This isn't over."

Wrath urged Mae to the door. "Wait for me just outside, Mae. I won't be long." That was a ploy to see if anyone would try to take her in the office -- if Barrison or Devo were brave enough to give the order for someone to try to grab Mae. In reality, Rycks and El Segador were at either end of the hall controlling traffic, as it were. No one was getting close to Mae without getting a beat-down. Didn't ease Justice's nerves. Watching the feed, he was wound tight as a banjo string, his gut churning at the thought of Mae in danger, especially with him not there to protect her.

"Mr. Barrison," Wrath said as he closed the door. When he turned around, the look on his face must have been something to behold, because Justice watched with satisfaction as both Barrison and Devo took a step backward, Devo knocking over his chair. "You have no idea who you're dealing with. Mae, while highly intelligent and dogged as any pit-bull lawyer I've ever met, isn't the real threat to you. She had one goal in mind. Freeing an innocent man. I, on the other hand, am a highly trained, highly skilled servant of the law. If you think you're in trouble because of what Mae dug up, keep pissing me off. I'll find every secret you've ever buried and bring them out into the harsh light of day. I've already started an investigation, and what I've uncovered is… well. It's not pretty. And not something you'd want finding its way onto the desk of anyone you can't control. Harass Miss Stephens or Mr. Creed anymore, and you'll be taking on a law firm you have no hope of controlling. Or buying off." He opened the door again, not bothering to ask if the two men understood the situation they were in. "Good day, gentlemen," he said, his voice booming in the office and down the hall. It was a signal to Rycks and El Segador he was taking charge of Mae and making his way to the exit. The other two men would clear a path in front of and behind them.

"What happened?" Mae asked softly as they got in the elevator. Wrath said nothing, only kept his eyes forward. Justice could see a fine tremor run through Mae and had to grind his teeth. He hated not being with her. He also hated the way Wrath was treating her. She was sensitive, dammit! He needed to be kinder.

"Not sure there's a kind bone in that man's body," Shotgun said, amusement tinging his voice. Justice hadn't meant to say that out loud, but then he'd never been this nervous before. Hell, he'd never been nervous a day in his life. Things simply were as they were.

"Well, he needs to find some. Especially if he's going to deal with Mae in any form."

"Brother, the woman took up with you. How fuckin' sensitive could she be?"

"Fucker."

* * *

"You said we had a rat in Salvation's Bane," Justice said. He and Rycks were having a beer while the women swam in the big pool in the back of the clubhouse. The whole yard was walled off with a privacy wall that was fortified with armed guards at each corner and in the middle of each wall. No one was fucking getting past the wall. Especially not when the women were outside the compound.

"Yeah. From what I've been able to piece together, he came about a year ago. I'm pretty sure he's feeding Kiss of Death every scrap of information he can get his hands on."

"Ain't much. Thorn has the actual club business locked down tight. He might be able to give them patched member movements, but I can't think of anything else. You know who his contact is?"

"No. But a friend of ours, Azriel Ivanovich, is pretty sure this Rat Man at Kiss of Death is either a current or former member of the Brotherhood."

"Hum..." Justice rubbed his chin thoughtfully as he turned his attention back to Mae in that bright red string bikini she was wearing. Wet, it clung to her like a second skin. Her nipples poked out, just beckoning him to suck them. If she climbed the steps out of the pool, he was sure the bottom would disappear between her cheeks and the outline of her pussy lips would be clearly visible. "I've heard of them. Secretive. Not many even know the name, let alone anyone involved with them."

"You know anything about them?"

Justice glanced at Rycks. "Besides that Ivanovich used to be a member but managed to sever all ties to them? Until recently, he had no contact with them. Then his partner, Alexi Petrov, had woman troubles and the Brotherhood showed up to entertain some of their guests. That was several years ago. But my understanding is that Azriel didn't make such a clean break the second time. I think your man El Diablo is also a former member. Though, I hear he still takes an odd job for them now and then. How exactly does that work anyway?" Didn't really answer the question, but Justice wasn't in the mood right now.

"That, my friend, is beyond your need to know."

Justice shrugged. "Can't blame a guy for askin'." He took a pull from his beer. "So you don't know exactly who our rat is?"

"No. But we're committed to helping you find out."

"Out of the goodness of your heart." Justice couldn't keep the sneer from his voice or his face. "Not buyin' that, Rycks. El Diablo don't strike me as the generous sort."

"Besides his daughter and her man's club, Bones, El Diablo has found he has a fondness for all of you. He just wants to help. Mae is now part of Bane, so he considers Bane one of the fold, so to speak."

"Kinda what I'm afraid of," Thorn said, taking a seat beside the two men. "We might be a pet project to El Diablo, but we ain't one of his fold. Bane's my club. Not his."

Rycks sat back, scrubbing his hand over his eyes wearily. "That's not the way it is, Thorn. I don't know how to say this in a way you can understand, and I'm not really sure how much El Diablo wants you to know, so I'll just put it like this. El Diablo thinks of all of you as family with him as… not the head, but like the patriarch. Bane and Bones do their own thing, but when they need help or when trouble comes their way, El Diablo sees it as his job to get involved. Kinda of like big brother stepping in."

"Then he's crazier than I thought."

"I'm not done, and I'm not doing a very good job of this," Rycks muttered. "He doesn't have many friends. No family other than Magenta. With finding Magenta and having to accept her man as part of another club, the very club he intended on taking over, he took it as a sign or something. Bones imprinted on him and then Salvation's Bane. He has no animosity toward you. I can't tell you how he feels or what his intentions are. I believe he wants us all three to function independently but be one when it's necessary. Kind of like, you mess with one of us, you mess with all of us."

Thorn looked thoughtful. "I can see the merit. But you're right. You can't speak for him. Until I look into his eyes while he tells me himself, there's nothing for us to discuss."

"There would be advantages," Justice mused. He glanced at Thorn. "And it would mesh with some of the things I've heard the last few years." It was all Justice was willing to say in front of Rycks, but Thorn got the message. There was definitely room for an alliance of sorts. Assuming El Diablo didn't have his own agenda, which was certainly possible. Nothing was too elaborate for the man. The only way to be secure in that kind of relationship was just to throw caution to the wind and trust the man. And Justice just wasn't there yet.

"In the meantime," Rycks continued, "I'm willing to help flush out your rat."

"Ain't bustin' him until we get all of 'em," Thorn said. "I want to take down the whole fuckin' bunch. Rat Man will be the message. But, if he's reporting to the Brotherhood, we need to have a plan. And we need to know why he'd be interested in us."

"I can only guess he's wanting a way into Black Reign, but that's speculation."

"You think our rat is thinkin' that far ahead?" It

was easy to see the wheels turning in Thorn's mind, working out all the angles.

"No," Rycks said immediately. "I think your rat is personal. In fact, if I were you, I'd check your ranks for a disgruntled member. Or former member."

"Why? What makes you think that?"

"Because we don't have a clue who it is." Justice saw the logic. "That's the only way someone gets into Salvation's Bane without you knowing it, Thorn. It's someone you trust. Figure out who you've pissed off and why. Then nail the motherfucker."

"If it's members, it'll be a short list. We'll have to dig deeper."

"I'll see what I can come up with." Justice was only half paying attention. He knew the problem now. What to do about it. Hell, he even knew where to start. Now he was focused on his woman. Mae was getting out of the pool and that swimsuit was, indeed, clinging to every nook and cranny of her body. At least, where it covered her. There was a lot of skin showing. A lot of skin…

The other two men continued to talk, but Justice had his mind on other things. He stood and moved up behind Mae, then wrapped his arms around her from behind. She squealed, but laughed and leaned her wet body against him.

"I'm getting you all wet." God, her laughter was musical.

"So, strip me. Dry me off."

She grinned back over her shoulder. "I think I can manage that."

* * *

Mae couldn't remember a time in her life when she'd been happier. Not only was Justice the most wonderful man with her, but he'd started helping her study to get into law school. Turned out, she was dyslexic. She'd refused help from Rycks, thinking she just wasn't cut out for school, but when Bones got involved with the tightening of security at Salvation's Bane and Cain had made the trip to Florida with his wife, Angel, the other woman had figured out almost immediately what was wrong. Thank goodness, Angel was a teacher. She knew enough about Mae's problem to help her figure out how to help herself, and things had snowballed.

The only problem she had was that she'd started to gain weight. Probably because she was truly happy. With that came a raging appetite. As a result, she'd started working out. Thankfully, Salvation's Bane owned a gym in Palm Beach. Beach Fit had personal trainers and the most modern equipment. Admittedly, Mae was addicted to the things Justice provided for her. But mostly, she was just addicted to Justice.

A few days ago, Justice had given her a thin chain with a tiny medallion on it. There was a small stone set in a thin layer of gold. When he'd fastened it around her neck, the setting had nestled in the hollow of her throat. He hadn't said anything, just put it on her and kissed her temple.

"You ready to go?" Slash was her escort today. Usually, if Justice couldn't be with her, he put Venus on her. Mae loved Venus. The woman was a serious badass in hot pink. Slash was nice enough, but he was always hurrying her. It was obvious he didn't want to babysit her. Probably, he'd rather be with the patched members working out a way to turn their defense into some kind of offense. Justice said Slash was a promising prospect. He trusted the man, or he wouldn't have put him in charge of protecting Mae.

"Yeah," she answered. "You leading or

following?"

"I'll be on your six. I think Venus is waiting a mile up the road to lead us in."

"Oh, good. I'd hoped to talk to her today but figured she was in the big meeting."

Was it her imagination or did Slash's smile look more like a sneer? "She is. But they're done."

Mae got an uneasy feeling, but she just smiled and nodded, unlocking her car and climbing in. Slash started his bike and waited patiently for her to buckle her seat belt and put the car in gear. She hated to admit it -- and probably never would to Justice -- but Slash gave her the creeps. Had from the day she'd met him. Of course, not all men in Salvation's Bane were as tame as Justice.

Tame. Right.

She took off and tried to ignore everything else and just drive. Turning on Hair Nation on Sirius, she sang "Don't Go Away Mad (Just Go Away)" at the top of her lungs. The sea air blowing through the window invigorated her, making her anxious to get back to the clubhouse. If they were finished with their meeting, Justice would be free, and she could corner him in their room and have her wicked way with him.

Blue lights flashed behind her.

What the fuck? She glanced down at her speedometer. She was only doing fifty in the fifty-five miles-per-hour zone. There had been no stop lights or signs that she remembered. Did she have a busted taillight? Not likely. The club was meticulous about shit like that for this very reason. They didn't want the cops to have any reason to pull them over.

As she switched on her emergency flashers and eased to the curb, she kept glancing behind her, trying to see where Slash was. He'd probably hold back and contact the club, but Mae was surprised she didn't see him anywhere off in the distance. Maybe he was just staying low.

The cop was getting out of his car, and that spurred Mae into action. She leaned over to get her registration and proof of insurance out of the glove compartment and was about to go fishing in her purse for her license when the door of her car was yanked open. A meaty hand grabbed her upper arm in a vise-like grip.

"Hey! My registration --" The big guy squeezed her arm hard.

"Shut the fuck up!"

He pulled out a knife, and it was all Mae could do not to scream. Instead of stabbing her, he cut the seat belt and hauled her out of the car.

"I don't un-understand! What's going on?"

"You're under arrest," he snapped, whirling her around and shoving her roughly up against the car. Handcuffing her hands behind her back, the guy leaned in close to her. "Thought your little biker club could protect you, huh? How'd that work out for you?"

Mae froze. Oh, God! These were the people the DA's office -- or someone in it -- had hired to get their revenge. What was she going to do? And where was Slash?

Once the big man had her secured, he pulled her away from the car and practically dragged her to his squad car, shoving her into the back seat.

Two things she noticed immediately. First, the smell was ungodly. It was like someone had puked, pissed, and shit pure Jack Daniels right where her face landed. She scrambled to sit up, but the guy shoved her back down. This time, there was the barrel of a gun pressing into the back of her skull.

"Stay down, you fuckin' cunt! Or I'll blow your fuckin' brains out!"

"I can't... I can't stay down here."

The guy just kicked her feet in the door, then slammed it. Seconds later he was inside the car, starting it up even before the door was closed. Then he peeled out and took off down the road. Which was the second thing she'd noticed as she struggled to get a glimpse out of the front window. There was no cage separating her and the cop in the front seat. She'd bet her last dollar he wasn't a cop. Or if he was, he wasn't using his official vehicle.

"Where are you taking me?"

"I said to shut the fuck up!" The guy picked up his phone and stabbed it with his thumb a couple of times before putting it to his ear. "Yeah. Got the bitch. Be there in thirty."

A thirty-minute drive meant they were either booking it hard to Fort Lauderdale, or they were headed to a remote area somewhere in the swamp. Somehow, Mae wasn't betting on seeing Fort Lauderdale any time soon.

Chapter Seven

When he found that motherfucker Slash, Justice was going to dismember him. Slowly.

"Where they headed?" he barked into the headset in his helmet. Justice rarely wore one, but it was necessary to communicate with the club while riding his bike.

"Looks like straight into the swamp. One of those run-down shacks trappers use. It's been on our radar since we started this manhunt." Shotgun might not be the best at intel gathering, but he knew who to go to when necessary, and he'd had Bones intel people all over this since they'd determined there was a danger to Mae. "Pretty sure that's where they're headed."

"Don't like fuckin' pretty sure, Shotgun."

"I know. Which is why I'm continuing to follow them. Good thing you put that tracker on her. The necklace was a stroke of genius."

"You sure it'll pick them up out there? Cell service is spotty at best."

"It uses satellite. As long as they're outside, it will pick her up. I expect to lose signal when they get her inside unless she's by a window, so don't freak out on me."

"Fucker," Justice muttered.

It wasn't fifteen minutes later when Shotgun came back to him. "Lost her right where I should have. She's in that shack. One hundred percent."

"Hold up." Rycks voice came over the earpiece, calm and strong. "Are you absolutely certain they didn't use a decoy? Is there any possibility they found the tracker and are leading us away from her?"

There was a pause, probably Shotgun conferring with Data from Bones. When he finally answered, there was no hesitation in his voice. "Data says he's been assured by Giovanni something-or-other from Shadow Demons the tracker absolutely cannot be detected. Apparently, it's a prototype from Argent Tech."

"Good. We go, then." Rycks pulled up alongside Justice. It struck Justice how dissimilar he and the other man were. Rycks was refined, if just barely. But he also preferred to dress more upper class. And the bike he rode was a high-end crotch rocket. Not a big Harley. As fast as Justice could go when he needed to, Rycks could outrun him on the open road. They weren't headed into the open road.

It wasn't long before the road they were traveling went from pavement to gravel to dirt to… nothing. Fortunately, since they'd known about this place when Mae was taken, they'd also been prepared for it. The second the men shut down their bikes, they heard a rumbling in the distance as Red, the Salvation's Bane mechanic and Road Captain, sped toward them with the vehicles they needed.

When he skidded to a stop, mud flying everywhere, Justice moved to the trailer where he had the ATVs. "Get 'em unloaded," he called to Rycks. All three men unstrapped the machines from inside the trailer. Two Honda Talons with an arsenal of guns strapped to and inside the vehicle were backed out. Justice snagged an extra helmet and tossed it in the seat beside him.

"Extra ammo in the back," Poison said. Justice had missed the man completely in his haste to get to Mae. "Got some grenades and smoke bombs, too." Rycks climbed into the other Talon while Poison crouched down in the back, fiddling with a big gun he hauled up from the back and locked in place on the roll bar, effectively turning the thing into a mobile tactical unit.

Justice glanced at the others. All of them did one last check on their weapon of choice, then nodded. "Justice in Talon 1," he said, confirming his ride and that he'd be the lead into the hot zone."

"Rycks in Talon 2 with Poison up top."

"Copy that. Both Talons manned and ready." Shotgun would be their control. The guy they depended on to get them in and out safely. And to send reinforcements if necessary. "You've got GPS coordinates on your dashboard, along with a map with your route. Don't stray from it or you could find a sinkhole."

"Copy." Justice was ready to go. He had a pressing need to get to Mae and to destroy the fuckers who'd taken her. If they'd hurt her, the end wouldn't come quickly. They started up the Talons and, moments later, took off.

Finding the place wasn't difficult, despite the remoteness of the area and the natural obstacles of the swamp. Which was puzzling. Justice would have thought anyone from Bane who'd been involved with this would have defended the place better. It just reinforced the idea he'd been right. No way his brothers could have been involved, in Mae's kidnapping or the murder years earlier. They cleaned up their messes and they defended their holes in the earth so no one could find the screams even if they could hear them. He'd have to work it all out. Later.

They approached the stop point. They were close enough to go the rest of the way on foot, but far enough away that any noise from the Talons wouldn't seem like a threat. Rycks took his and circled the perimeter while Justice grabbed a side arm and an automatic rifle and made his way through the swamp.

"You're close, Justice." Shotgun's voice in his ear was at once annoying and comforting. Reminded Justice of his days in the military. He both loved and hated that big brother hovered over him at times. "Just a few hundred more feet."

"I see the top of the shack." Just as he said that, there was sharp scream followed by a female voice swearing. "Fuck!"

"Don't go in hot!" Rycks's voice was commanding. "Keep it down! Circle around and go in the back. There's a small window. You probably won't fit, but she will."

"If she can get to me. She's screaming, Rycks!"

"Give her some credit, Justice. Just do it as we planned. Don't deviate unless you actually see her in distress."

"How can you be so calm about this? They're hurting her!"

"Because she's my ward. Do you think I didn't teach her how to take care of herself?"

No. The other man would have definitely made sure the tiny Mae could take care of herself. Otherwise, he'd never have let her out of the fucking clubhouse. That was when he heard a shrill war cry that sounded suspiciously like Mae.

"Fuck it," Justice muttered.

He hurried around the shack to the back, just like Rycks told him. Inside, he could see Mae battling a guy easily twice her size and three times her weight. Guy was fucking huge! He backhanded Mae and she spun around, but Justice saw her snag a knife that had been lying on the table he'd knocked her into. Her hands were handcuffed in front of her, which was odd. He'd have thought they'd have bound her hands behind her back at the very least.

When she turned back around, the knife was concealed along her forearm. The guy stepped toward her and, just as he snagged her left arm, she lunged and drove the knife under his chin with a shrill scream. When she stepped back, the guy's eyes were wide, and he pawed at the knife still sticking out under his chin. Blood flowed down his neck onto the white T-shirt he wore. Sickening, strangled sounds came from the guy and blood bubbled from his lips.

Mae spat at the guy. "Motherfucker!" When he dropped to his knees, Mae kicked the knife with a hard, upward strike, embedding it as deep as it would go. When he fell and quit moving, she knelt beside him and shoved with all her might, groaning as she did.

"I'm going around front," Justice said. "Looks like she didn't need my help."

"Watch for traps," Rycks warned. The man didn't say, "I told you so," but it was implied.

Seconds later, Justice was in the front door only to find Mae unlocking her cuffs and spiking them on the dead guy's head. "Told you I'd fuck you up, you bastard."

"Anyone else here?" She crouched, reaching for the knife still embedded in her captor's throat, but Justice raised his empty hands. "Hey. Just me, princess."

"Archer!" She threw herself in his general direction and Justice wrapped his arms around her tightly. She was trembling and had started sobbing, but didn't flinch when he squeezed her tight. That was a good sign.

"You hurt?"

"Just where he slapped me. Mostly, I just need a fucking shower. The car they brought me here in was filthy."

"Come on." He grabbed her hand and they crept out of the shack. "You didn't answer me before. Is anyone else here?"

"One of the DAs. Devo. He was trying to get a hold of someone over him to decide what to do with me. I got the impression he was supposed to eliminate me but couldn't quite bring himself to do it. Kind of like… maybe I was an initiation? You know. Like they wanted to know he was all in, and killing me was the way to get him in deep so he couldn't get out."

"Makes sense. He plannin' on coming back?"

"I think so. When he does, he'll be alone. Probably with a way to kill me that won't look messy. He strikes me as squeamish."

Justice cupped her face in his hands. "You scared the life out of me."

"Hey. Wasn't my fault. I did everything I was supposed to do."

He pressed a gentle kiss to her lips. "We'll talk about it later. Right now, we need to get back to my ride and out of this fuckin' swamp." One more hard kiss, then he took out his extra pistol. "You know how to use one of these?"

Mae took it from him, ejected the clip and inspected it. Then she shoved it back in and chambered a round. She raised an eyebrow and gave him a look.

"Guess that answers that question."

"We going? 'Cause, I gotta tell you. This place gives me the creeps."

"Stick close. Step exactly where I step. We have a short walk to our ride, then we'll meet up with the others."

Together, they made their way back to the Talon. Justice stopped there for several minutes, surveying the area. "Stay here. I'm making a sweep around the area."

"You think they found it?"

"No. I'm just being careful."

"See that you are," she said, leaning up to kiss him once. "I'll be very put out if you aren't."

"You got it, princess."

Justice had no doubt the area was secure. He was just being extra careful. The last thing he wanted was to get either of them hurt this late in the game. Once he'd approached the Talon, he snagged his helmet, putting it on.

"This is Talon 1. I have her. Anything in our area?"

"That's a negative, Talon 1. Talon 2 reports no one in or out of the area. You're clear back to the rendezvous."

"We'll be there in fifteen. Be advised one for recycle. One bogey expected back."

"Understood."

He motioned for Mae, who darted out of the underbrush and to the Talon. He tossed her a helmet. "Hop in."

The ride out was as uneventful as it had been on the way in. As they approached Red and the trailer, Rycks and Poison merged behind them from the woods as if it had been choreographed that way. Rycks pulled his ride into the trailer first. While Poison was dismantling the top gun, Justice pulled his Talon in.

"Don't take off your helmet," he told Mae. "Get on my bike." She obeyed, waiting for him patiently while he secured the ATVs.

"Still feel like there's another shoe to drop," Rycks muttered, his eyes darting around them, searching.

"I can't disagree, though having her back with us

eases my mind considerably."

"Agreed. Keep your eyes open. Be aware. Anything seems off, we deal with it immediately. No matter how small."

"No arguments there." Justice stuck out his hand to Rycks. "Still don't like you."

Rycks took it, gripping his hand hard. "Ain't made up my mind about you either."

Justice slapped Rycks's arm before turning to his bike and Mae. "Rip it up, Rycks. Back to your clubhouse."

"I got your six." He nodded. "Rip it up."

Justice took it slower than he normally would. Not only was he not accustomed to the more off-road aspects of the ride out, but he didn't want to risk Mae losing her balance. Once they were on the pavement, though, he sped up. The quicker they could make it to the highway and the road home, the better he'd feel.

"Exiting the swamp," Rycks informed Shotgun.

"The boys are coming up behind you. Keep Mae in the middle. Expecting some company, though El Diablo has Wrath ready for 'em."

Wrath. That meant visitors of the legal kind. Which was just fine with Justice. He was ready to punch a motherfucker in the face. He only hoped it was that pissant Devo.

Fifteen minutes later, they pulled into the Black Reign compound. Sure enough, there were two cop cars and a black sedan. Was that all they had or were Devo and Barrison holding back some heavy hitters?

The boys in front rolled the group toward the garage, but one of the cop cars backed in front of them, blocking the way. Samson was the lead bike, the Road Captain for this particular run since Red was hanging back with the trailer and the Talons. Even though they hadn't fired a shot, they didn't want the cops to have a look at the equipment. Some of the ordnance was questionable at best. Samson stopped, but revved his bike loudly. Justice could just imagine the heavy scowl he gave the officer, who didn't get out of the car.

El Diablo raised a hand and Samson immediately stopped, shutting off his bike and getting off. The others followed suit. Justice was last to dismount. He made a show of helping Mae from his bike and taking her helmet from her.

"Justice," El Diablo called, waving him to the font of the house. "Bring little Mae to me."

Justice had an uneasy feeling, but he couldn't outright defy El Diablo in his own compound. He noticed Cain and Vicious from Bones were there, as well as Tobias and Stryker from Salvation's Bane. While Bones might not have any other representatives with them, Justice knew Bane was well represented. If there were two of them, there were more.

"She wants a shower and a change of clothes," Justice said, ignoring everyone but El Diablo.

"Looks as if she had some trouble." El Diablo raised an eyebrow and slowly reached out to Mae, tracing a finger lightly over the reddish bruise forming on her cheek. "I trust this was taken care of."

"Mae had things well in hand when I picked her up." Justice was careful how to word himself, not wanting to give anything away in the presence of the enemy.

"Go, then," El Diablo told Mae. "Take your time. I'll send Justice up to you when we're done."

"I appreciate it," she said. "But I'd like to stay." Her gaze was on a figure getting out of the back of the sedan. Devo. On her face was a look of pure hatred. No doubt she had her own dark thoughts. Justice wanted to kick the guy's ass. Or worse.

El Diablo chuckled. The sound... wasn't pleasant. "I always knew I liked you, little Mae."

"Believe in standing my ground."

"So you should. Stand with Justice, then. You stood for him before. Now he can stand for you."

Justice put his hand on her shoulder and squeezed. She looked back at him with a sweet smile. When she turned back to face the men from the DA's office, the expression on her face was anything but sweet.

"State your business," El Diablo said, crossing his arms over his chest.

"We were here to, uh, make sure Mae was OK." Devo tugged at the collar of his shirt several times, swallowing nervously before adjusting his tie. "We understand her car was found on the side of the road. Given that she's been with a dangerous criminal recently --" He glanced at Justice. "-- we wanted to make sure she wasn't hurt."

"Oh, I got hurt," she muttered just loud enough for everyone to hear. "Might have been hurt worse if I hadn't declined to stay in the company I was with."

Wrath stepped in front of her then. "Gonna need that warrant, Barrison," he called loudly. A few seconds later, the man in question stepped from the back of the car, a wide smile on his face.

"Mae. I'm so happy to see you're all right. When the city's officers reported your car on the side of the road, we feared the worst."

"Find it hard to believe you'd worry over one woman out of all of them in the city," Wrath said. "Especially one who brought your department such grief. One could almost infer you were here to confirm her disappearance. Wishful thinking?" He stalked down the stairs, one boot at a time. "Or something more sinister."

"I'm not sure what you're implying, Vincent, but my motives were pure. I simply wanted to make sure the girl hadn't met any trouble."

Mae was going to spout off. Justice could see it as her face darkened in anger. Squeezing her shoulder, he tried to warn her to keep silent.

"Horseshit," Wrath spat. "You're a fuckin' liar, Barrison."

The man only shrugged. "If you say so. I still need to do a wellness check of Mae. Alone."

"Not happenin'," Wrath said decisively.

Barrison pulled out a piece of paper, an evil smile on his face. "I'm afraid it is, Vincent. This is a warrant allowing us to do a wellness check on one Mae Stephens."

Wrath snatched the paper from Barrison and scanned it. Then he snorted. "Sure. It allows you to enter the premises and check on her. Well --" He waved a hand in Mae's direction. "-- there she is. You want a one-on-one with her, you will do it here. And she will have a person of her choosing present."

"I want Wrath with me," Mae said instantly. "He's my lawyer, and I have the right to have my lawyer with me when being questioned by the police, or anyone working for the justice system. Also, I'd like to point out that I don't feel safe with you or any of your officers. If that's a problem, then I go to the police station with my lawyer and we'll discuss it there." She took a step forward. "But under no circumstances will I be anywhere alone with you."

"I'm afraid you have no choice, my dear."

El Diablo pulled his side arm, chambering a round and pointing the gun straight at Barrison. All around him, the same sounds of guns going to the ready filled the air. Justice cringed.

"It's the fucking O.K. Corral," he muttered. "Whatever happens, stay behind me."

"My suggestion," El Diablo said pleasantly, "is that you execute your warrant in a different manner. We'll risk contempt of court or whatever charge the judge sees fit, but Mae is not going with you."

Wrath took out his phone and stabbed a button, making a call. He put it to his ear and waited. A couple of seconds later, he spoke to the person on the other end. "Release it," he said in a clipped voice. "Barrison. Hold the others. Call me when it's done."

Barrison tilted his head, his eyes narrowing. "Don't threaten me, Vincent. I'll bury you."

"I don't threaten. I made you a promise at our last meeting. I was just following through."

There was a beat of silence. Barrison looked at Wrath warily. "What did you do?"

"You'll find out shortly. Get your affairs in order, Barrison. I'd say you have an hour at most." Wrath backed up the steps, putting himself between the DA and Mae. Barrison sputtered and demanded the officers take her into custody, but the men of Salvation's Bane, Black Reign, and Bones could be intimidating when they wanted to be. Would there be trouble later? Justice was sure of it. He also knew neither El Diablo nor Wrath did something like this without a plan. Chances were, whatever Wrath had on Barrison was enough to make this incident insipid by comparison.

Just before Wrath got them to the door, Barrison's phone rang. He glanced at it, annoyed. Then his face paled. He answered it and slowly brought it to his ear.

"Barrison." His voice was husky. Nervous.

Another phone rang. This one was from one of the officers. He brought the phone to his ear and said nothing, just listened. His gaze snapped to El Diablo, then Wrath. Finally, he just said, "Understood." He nodded to one of his partners, who shoved Devo into the back seat of the car. When Devo tried to get out, the officer slammed the door against him two times in hard, rapid succession, then shoved the man more forcefully into the vehicle and shut the door.

"What's going on here?" Barrison put his phone in his pocket and turned his full attention to the officers around him. "We need to take her back to the DA's office."

"I'm afraid that's not what's happening," the lead officer said. "You have a meeting with Mr. Malcolm."

Barrison's knees gave out and he would have fallen, but the other two officers caught him under the arms. They literally dragged his dead weight to the other side of the car.

"Call him back!" Barrison yelled. "Call him back! I told him I had this taken care of and he was good!"

"You'll learn that dealing with Malcolm is seldom what you think," El Diablo said to Barrison. The other man's eyes were wild, desperate, as they shoved his head down and his body into the car. The officer closed the door and got into the front passenger side. The sound of the locks clicking into place was loud in the silence around them. Justice found it amusing that, of all the people in that yard, the District Attorney was the one making all the noise. The bikers were eerily silent.

The officer in charge turned to El Diablo. "I don't know who you people are, but normally, Malcolm would have me deal with you all as well. He told me going in we were not to lay a hand on anyone in the club but the girl. Now, even that order has changed." He nodded to Mae. "He said to consider her off limits. She's safe from his organization."

"Tell Malcolm this isn't even a start on repayment of his debt to me. Nevertheless, I'll still hold him to it. Little Mae is not to be harmed. If she is, her protector will be unleashed."

"Protector?"

El Diablo grinned. "Well, protector is a bit of an understatement. She's Justice's property. My advice would be to harm her at your own risk."

"Justice." The cop turned to look at Wrath, Mae, and Justice where they stood in front of the door. Wrath looked back over his shoulder, not liking the attention in their direction, but Justice wasn't hiding behind anyone. The only reason he'd stayed there so long was to make sure he could drag Mae inside if necessary.

Now, he moved around the other two, standing as proud and tall as he ever had in the prison yard to intimidate anyone from gang members to the guards.

"I'm Justice," he said. "And the Brotherhood is getting a reputation on the inside. It's not a good one. I don't know much about them, but Joaquin Malcolm, I know."

The cop tilted his head. "Archer Creed. Justice."

"That's me."

"You got quite a reputation in prison. Caught the notice of some people."

"I'm fully aware of that," Justice acknowledged. "You should know that I never do anything by chance. If I got noticed, it was intentional."

The guy nodded. "He said that about you.

Warned me off you for my own good."

"Sounds like Malcolm has a use for you."

"Maybe. Maybe I have a use for him."

That made Justice chuckle. "Don't delude yourself into thinking he needs you more than you need him. You saw how quickly he cut off Barrison and Devo. You can go just as easily."

"Perhaps. The difference between me and them, though, is that I follow my instructions. To the letter. He says do something, I do it. These guys think they own Malcolm. I know it's the other way around, and I'm good with it. He makes me rich."

"As long as you realize the hand that feeds you can also put a bullet in your brain."

The officer smiled. "I'm fully aware. Which is why I do my best to make myself indispensable. I do what he says when he says with no questions. I'm fully loyal to Malcolm. Not the Brotherhood. Malcolm."

El Diablo chuckled softly. "Words like that will certainly get you killed, young man. You're in over your head. My advice is to not get too close to anyone. That way, when they kill you, it's only yourself you have to worry about."

That made the guy pause, but he said nothing. Only got into the driver's side, started the car, and took off.

"Get your woman inside and settled. I believe she wanted a shower? Once you're satisfied she's good, come to my office," El Diablo instructed.

Justice hated taking orders from anyone, but this was necessary.

"Go on, Archer." Mae slid her arms around his neck. "I'll be upstairs in our room waiting for you."

Automatically, Justice returned the embrace, holding her tightly against him. He could have lost her today. "I don't want to leave you."

She found his mouth with hers, licking softly. "You're not. We're in this house together. No one is going to bother me. Go see what El Diablo has to say, then come to me."

Reluctantly, he let her go. He watched her until she disappeared around the corner on the second-story landing. Then he took a deep breath. Dealing with El Diablo under the best of circumstances wasn't his forte. This was going to be torture.

Chapter Eight

Justice was just about to follow Wrath inside El Diablo's office when the front door opened and in walked Slash, of all people. Justice saw red. Without a word, he stalked toward the prospect. Faster and faster with each step. Just as Slash turned his head in Justice's direction, Justice reached out and took the younger man by the throat and slammed him up against the wall. Slash tried to claw, kick, and punch his way free, but Justice used his elbow, slamming it into the kid's cheek. A gash ripped open after the third blow. His head hit the wall so hard, blood smeared where Slash's scalp split.

"You had one job, you little motherfucker. One fuckin job!"

"Hey, man! I lost her in traffic! I tried to catch up, but the cops already had her. I stayed back like Rycks taught us, but I lost them. I looked for her before comin' back here for help. Did you guys find her?"

"And that took you four fuckin' hours?" With a brutal yell, Justice slammed his fist into Slash's face two times before backing off completely. Several of Black Reign had stopped what they were doing and watched avidly. None of them offered to help either man. Probably didn't care much if two members of another club beat each other down. "I see you again, you little bastard, I'll fuckin' kill you."

Slash gave him an angry sneer. "Oh, you'll see me again," he muttered. "I'll fuckin' make you bleed."

Justice learned in prison never to make threats. You did or you didn't. He also learned to not let threats go unchecked. You never wanted something hanging over your head.

So he beat Slash to a bloody pulp. It was long

and violent and right there in the common room of the clubhouse of another club. No one stopped him until the very end when Rycks laid a hand on his shoulder.

"Can't let you kill him, Justice."

Justice gave Slash one last, vicious kick to the ribs. The man didn't move. He looked back at Rycks, then found Thorn across the room. His president was tight-faced with disapproval. Of him or Slash, Justice wasn't sure.

"Bastard's got more comin'."

"No," Thorn said. "He deserved what he got, but this is enough. We'll take up his continued prospect status when we get back home, but for now, he's still a prospect with Salvation's Bane. "El Diablo, we'd appreciate it if Fury could tend to Slash."

"Young man is most definitely in need of medical attention," El Diablo said. His voice held no inflection. If anything, he sounded completely disinterested in Slash's predicament. "I will say, Justice was justified in what he did. Your prospect should never have let little Mae drive herself, no matter how much he wanted to ride his bike. It's a mistake, I assume, he'll never get the chance to repeat."

"Damn straight," Justice said, looking at Thorn. "We can't trust our prospects, they can't be prospects."

"You don't get to decide that, Justice." Now, Thorn was all business. The president of their club. "The club decides who is and who is not a prospect. As a whole. You don't want to be part of that process, fine. But you don't get to dictate how I run things."

"I'd say there was always room for you at Black Reign, but I have to agree with your president on this." El Diablo was a smug bastard. If Justice wasn't mistaken, the man was enjoying the tiff between him and Thorn. "Besides, stealing Bane's best members is hardly a way to get Thorn to agree to an alliance. Mae will always be welcomed here. You, on the other hand, are contingent on your standing within Salvation's Bane."

"Don't need your help here, El Diablo." Thorn shot the man an annoyed look.

El Diablo raised his hands in a non-threatening gesture. "I'm only making sure your man knows the score. He and Mae are a couple, but he's not a part of Black Reign."

"Get in here," Thorn growled at Justice. "Let's get this done so you can get back to your woman. I'm sure she'll need your reassurance."

Justice watched as Vicious and Arkham hefted the unconscious Slash into a standing position, supporting him with his arms over their shoulders, and dragged him out of the room. Probably to the infirmary. Let Slash deal with the doctor named Fury and all his needles.

Justice followed Thorn, Cain, and El Diablo into an office in the back of the room. The space was richly decorated, more fit for a high-powered executive than an MC president. Leather and oak furniture, elaborate paintings, and a rich, thick rug complemented the massive desk situated in the corner of the room. El Diablo took his place behind the desk and regarded Thorn.

"You've got a problem, Thorn. That prospect will make Justice's life miserable, and, by extension, yours."

"Then he won't last long. I don't put up with bullshit."

Cain looked on passively, but Justice could almost see the wheels turning in his mind. There was a reason El Diablo had both presidents in the room. Justice just wasn't sure why he was there himself.

El Diablo looked at Justice. For the first time, Justice could see through the veneer of civility El Diablo projected. The man was a straight-up killer. He'd known that, but this was the first time he could actually put the man together with the myth. "What do you know of the Brotherhood?"

"I know you're confirming my suspicion that you've not severed ties as completely as you'd have Azriel Ivonovich believe."

There was a deadly silence in the room. Thorn cleared his throat. "Is there something here I should know? Because I hate being in the fuckin' dark on important things."

"Ditto," Cain agreed.

"Your man here appears to know things that could get him, and all of Salvation's Bane, killed. Quite possibly Bones as well, just because the two clubs often work closely together." El Diablo didn't answer Thorn with malice or intent, just with the facts as he saw them. At least, that was the way Justice perceived it. He knew enough about El Diablo to know that the man didn't threaten. He hit you before you knew there was a reason to be threatened.

"You're really pissing me off, El Diablo." Thorn stood. "If we're done, I've got shit to do."

"We're not," El Diablo said softy, never taking his gaze from Justice. "This needs to be said between us three. No one else." He glanced at Thorn. "Not even your wife must know this, but you need to. It could be the thing that saves all of you."

"Not likin' this. Justice. What have you been hidin'?"

"Ain't hidin' anything. I never did any diggin' into the Brotherhood. At least, not much. Whenever their name was mentioned, I paid attention. They're not the sort of people you want knowing you're lookin' into them." Justice sat back on the leather couch. The subject matter was uncomfortable enough. Might as well take advantage of what El Diablo was offering at the moment.

"The Brotherhood is complicated," he began. "From what I found out when looking into El Diablo's past after he took over Black Reign, they are shrouded in mystery and they prefer it that way. El Diablo here was their... enforcer. Only it was more complicated than that."

"I was their last avenue. Their final defense. Or their ultimate offense." El Diablo grinned, seeming to enjoy the attempt to regulate him to one job.

"You were their assassin," Justice supplied. "And from what I can tell, you never stopped."

El Diablo's face hardened. "I left them at great peril to myself and to Magenta. My association with the Brotherhood meant I could never have a relationship with her or her mother if I wanted them to be safe. Any failure on my part would be death for everyone I loved. Before they let me die myself." He glanced at Cain and Thorn. "I don't come without my own demons, but I've managed to find a balance with my former associates. They only contact me in dire situations, and I keep my secrets to myself."

"Are our clubs in danger because of our association with you?" Thorn brought the most pressing concern to the table. Justice could tell by the look on Cain's face he already knew the answer.

"The short answer is yes," Cain said, his gaze firmly on El Diablo. "But we were there already. With Justice claiming Mae, who is Rycks's ward, who is tightly associated with El Diablo, Salvation's Bane will be in the same jeopardy, if you keep Justice with you."

"You know what, Cain?" Justice stood, still itching for a fight. "Fuck you."

"Hey, I never suggested he sever ties. I was just laying it out there."

"Relax, Justice. I ain't cuttin' you loose."

"This is horseshit!" Justice paced across the room. "Mae is all I'm worried about. I can't keep her safe if I'm on my own."

"Calm your tits, Justice. You're not on your own." Sure, it had been several years, but Justice could tell Thorn was annoyed in the highest degree. "Now, sit the fuck down."

"Finish with what you know," El Diablo commanded. And it was nothing short of a command. An order given from a general to a private.

"Like I said, I didn't dig. I value my life too much. The Brotherhood is the apex of the crime world. They control…" Justice lifted his hands before letting them both fall back to his lap. "Everything. I mean literally everything. Every crime boss you've ever heard of, past and present, answers to them in some form. Any who've tried to pull away from them have been taken down. Hard. El Chapo tried to pull away. He isn't dead yet so I'm assuming they brought him in line. Al Capone, John Gotti… they all answered to the Brotherhood. Until they didn't."

"Not understanding how they have that much pull."

"Because they are a tight-knit group, loyal only to each other," El Diablo said. "It's not about the money for them. It's about power. At least, it is now. There was a time when their purpose was to keep those types of men in check. Sometime after I joined, the transition started from protecting the innocent to taking their piece of the pie. It's why I wanted out."

"Still not seeing how they could hold together that long. You're talking a hundred years." Cain wasn't buying it, Justice could tell.

"Longer." Justice whispered. "They've existed for longer than America has been a country. Started in England to keep the King and the Church in check. They're part of the reason America is America."

"It goes back further than that even. Much, much further." El Diablo sighed. "They changed over time and that's what makes them dangerous now. They're just as greedy now as those they once hunted. Which makes them vastly more powerful. Until they start to fight amongst themselves and squabble for money and power, they will continue to be a danger to everyone who knows about them."

"Why are you telling us this?" Thorn stood and took up Justice's pacing. "Seems to me like we might already be fucked."

"Quite the contrary," El Diablo said. "I believe you're safe for now. Assuming Justice doesn't let on how much he knows. They're looking to acquire Argent Tech and ExFil."

That got Cain to shoot to his feet. "Fuck," he muttered.

"Argent Tech," Justice said. "Shadow Demons. Azriel Ivonovich's company. I can understand that, but why ExFil?"

"Because we use many of the prototypes Argent creates," Cain supplied. "We are unique in our success in no small part due to Argent. No paramilitary organization in the world can do what we do."

"I believe they want Bones and Salvation's Bane as their personal army." El Diablo sat back in his chair. "At least, until they can train their own people and take over Argent."

"They tried once already," Thorn said. "Shadow Demons shut it down."

"True. But Azriel will tell you that won't be the end of it. The only thing saving Argent currently is that they are just as loyal to each other as the Brotherhood is to themselves."

"So, what do we do?" Justice asked.

"You think about what we've all learned here today. You take Mae home to her sister and start your lives together." El Diablo smiled, but it looked tired. "Then you decide if you want to ally with Black Reign."

"Rycks said you're not wanting control of the clubs." Justice didn't trust El Diablo as far as he could throw him, but he wanted to give Rycks the benefit of the doubt. If the man was lying, Justice couldn't tell it. It was a disadvantage, and he intended to start working that out.

El Diablo's gaze snapped to Justice. "He told you that?"

"Told me you wanted the three of us to work together, but independently. Kind of like we've been doing, only more formally."

"Well, he only got it partially right," El Diablo muttered. "I want Shadow Demons in with us. They're the key. If they agree, then we might be able to hold our own with the Brotherhood."

"Why are you so set against them now?" Cain jumped in. He'd known El Diablo longer than any of them except Azriel. "You worked for them. Killed for them. What changed you?"

"Because the organization I joined has been perverted. It was leaning that way when they recruited me, but they're nothing but the ultimate crime syndicate now. They don't even try to pretend they're protecting humanity. They want to rule the world. Argent Tech and ExFil are only two pieces of the puzzle for them. Large pieces, but pieces nonetheless. It may take decades, or even a century, but their ultimate goal is world domination. I joined to better protect humanity."

He looked down at his hands. "I gave up Magenta for them. Her mother was never someone I would have stayed with, but I still tried to move heaven and earth to protect Magenta. These young women Rycks has dedicated himself to are the same. They are women who were hurt but had heart and inner strength. Rycks saw something in them he needed to nurture. I have those same protective instincts, and they all started with finding Magenta. I've done things she'll never know about. My soul is stained beyond redemption. But those I consider mine I protect to the death. I think the three of you feel the same way. The Brotherhood goes against the very idea of family outside their ranks. All they want or need is power."

He sighed, scrubbing his hand over his eyes a few times. "I just want my family to survive this. Magenta. Mae. Justice and Sword by extension. Bones and Salvation's Bane as well. You see the domino effect? Azriel I feel a kinship for because he had the courage to break away before I did. I was gone but used the excuse of needing solitude to hide my intent. If I care for Azriel…"

"Then you need to include Shadow Demons," Cain finished. "Can't promise anything, but I'll talk with Alexi. Torpedo and I will discuss this at length before bringing it to the club."

"Same with me and Havoc," Thorn said. "We'll keep it to patched members only, as always."

"Find that mole," El Diablo said. "He or she is close."

"She?" Thorn was taken aback. "You mean a club girl?"

El Diablo shrugged. "Club girl. Ol' lady. It's painful, but you need to consider all options."

Thorn pointed a finger at El Diablo. "You're a fuckin' psychopath!"

"Sociopath, but who's squabbling? I'm not saying not to trust your wives. I'm just saying you need to look at everything and everyone. If there is a patched member you've found yourself questioning but dismissing because he's Salvation's Bane, take a closer look."

"Fuck." Cain gripped Thorn's shoulder. "Let's just get the fuck outta here and lick our wounds in private."

Thorn glared once more at El Diablo, then left. Justice followed. He needed to collect Mae and get the fuck out of this place. He'd grown too comfortable here. As a result, he found himself actually believing what El Diablo said.

Fuck. Just... fuck!

* * *

"So, it's official," Cain said, getting up from his place at the head of the table. He had nothing to do with Salvation's Bane's everyday business, but he was president of Bones. Though they were sister clubs, Cain was the acknowledged leader by simple virtue of being everyone's boss in ExFil. "We will have a loose alliance with Black Reign."

"Still don't trust that motherfucker," Sword said. He and Magenta had flown down at Magenta's insistence, eager to see her father on what she had deemed an important day.

"Not sure any of us do," Cain acknowledged. "But he makes valid points and everything he's said has been corroborated by Justice."

Thorn spoke up. "My gut says he's legit. I'm ninety-five percent sure of Rycks as well. I think that, if nothing else, he's got the best interests of his wards at heart."

"I'm also convinced he'd never do anything to put a woman in jeopardy if he could help it." Though Justice hated speaking up for Rycks on principle alone, he had to give the man that. He was even more protective than Justice was when it came to women. "Keep an eye on him, though," he cautioned. "Some vulnerable woman out there is going to be his downfall."

"And it could bring hell down on our clubs," Thorn finished. "Cain. Gonna need Data to give Shotgun a crash course in what you do. Get him any equipment he needs."

"I'll take some of that equipment, too." Ripper raised his hand, his face lighting up. "Want the good shit from Argent." Everyone chuckled.

"Done." Cain grinned and stood up. "Anything else before Bones leaves?"

"Keep a strong watch on your place," Thorn said quietly. "You're the most vulnerable of us. You're strong, but it would take time for anyone to get to you, isolated as you are."

"Noted. Been meaning to start work on a landing zone. Permits will be a bitch, but I'm betting Giovanni can help with that."

"If the hotshot tech behind Argent Tech can't do it, ask for Suzie's help." Justice wasn't sure who that came from, but everyone in the room erupted in laughter, dispelling the tension they'd had up until then.

"Gonna tell Giovanni you said that." Cain grinned, then reached out his hand to Thorn.

"Thanks for the hospitality, friend." Thorn took his hand and shook it hard.

"Anytime. Staying for the party?"

Cain grinned. "First party with the new club? Wouldn't miss it."

Enthusiastic agreements all around. The single men looked forward to the girls. The taken men looked forward to showing off their women. Everyone just wanted to party and let their guard down a while.

First thing Justice did was find out who was on guard duty. The combination of Shadow, Wrath, Trench, Samson, Lock, and Poison gave him great satisfaction. Two from each club with personalities that complemented each other. If nothing else, Shadow was perfectly capable of bringing them all together.

Eight o'clock rolled around and so did Black Reign. Harleys and a few crotch rockets littered the parking lot of the clubhouse. Music blared from the speakers, and the grills were going wide open. All kinds of grilled meats were being turned out, from burgers and hotdogs to chicken and shrimp. It still barely kept up with the ravenous appetite of the three clubs. At one point, Isadora brought out a whip and dared anyone near the grill for thirty minutes so she could get a little bit ahead.

"Wait a minute," one of the Black Reign men said suspiciously. "You're that chick what's a Domme at the Playground. I seen you!" The guy had a decidedly Cottony accent.

Isadora put her shoulders and her chin back, looking regal as any queen. "I am. And if you get near my grill before I say, I will flay your skin from your bones as easily as I did fish. We'll set up a little display. I have a St. Andrew's cross in my room."

The guy had stumbled backward, looking for all the world as if he faced a pack of rabid hell hounds. Then he turned an odd shade of green before stumbling to the nearest trashcan and emptying the contents of his stomach to the roar of laughter of everyone around.

Isadora sighed. "Must have seen my work on that scum trying to sneak in from Kiss of Death." She shook her head. One of the club girls, Trixie, giggled as she handed her an over-large set of tongs.

"You have to admit. That sight was a spectacle."

Isadora shrugged. "No more than the one Venus put on."

The woman in question, Venus, stretched where she lay on a nearby lounger with three men around her, vying for her attention. "I don't put on spectacle," she said in her sexy Russian accent. The woman knew how to work a crowd. "I simply walk through place. Men watch." She shook her head. "Not spectacle."

"Honey, you're a walking, talking spectacle. 'Cause, I mean, you stand out. Pink is one thing. Head to toe in hot pink? That's something else entirely."

Venus raised a hand to one of the guys, scrunching her nose like she would when making faces at a baby. Or a particularly cute puppy. She scratched him under the chin, her razor-sharp nails drawing thin lines of blood. The guy winced, but sighed happily. Venus brought her fingers to her mouth as if to lick them, then dropped her hand. The guy pouted, and she made a disgusted noise. "Pussy," she muttered. "How did pussy get in club? Are you spying for KoD?"

The guy looked affronted, but, oddly, interested. "If I say I am will you scratch me again?"

Venus rolled her eyes. "Blood whores can be annoyingly tenacious when they want to bleed." She shoved the guy back and stood.

The other men around her growled. One of them approached the blood whore and grabbed him by the throat and shoved him back into the fencing. He said something, then shoved the guy back and stalked away. Toward Venus. Who was currently swishing her hips and dragging those razor-sharp nails of hers over anyone stupid enough, or kinky enough, to get too close.

Beside him, Mae giggled. "You think that's funny?" Justice tried to sound put out, but he found it amusing as well.

"It's totally funny. What's even worse are the two men following her. Do you think she even noticed them?"

"Most women I'd say no. Venus? Yeah. She knows. Very little going on around her she doesn't notice."

"She's badass. Maybe I'll take some tips from her." Mae wiggled her fingers in front of his face. "Think I could get nails like hers?

"Paint them as pink as you want, but I'd rather you not stab me when you're hangin' on to me while I fuck you."

She giggled again. "You say the sweetest things."

Epilogue

As darkness fell, club members built bonfires around the massive yard they'd cleared a few years. Justice had no doubt that by morning there'd be more. Smaller maybe, but more. Some of those fires had women dancing around them in various stages of undress. Others were having sex out in the open with club girls or their ol' ladies. Justice was pretty sure he saw Stryker and Glitter and Vicious and Lucy putting on a show for everyone to watch. Since Stryker had taken Glitter, the two couples had been trying to outdo each other with the public sex. Both women seemed happy as fuck. The men sure as shit were.

"You think everything will be OK?" Mae said in a soft voice.

Had Justice not been so attuned to her, he might not have heard her. She was worried. "Yeah. I think so."

"What about the mole? Do you know who it is?"

"Got an idea. Nothing for you to worry about, princess. I've got this."

She looked up at him, serious now. "It is something for me to worry about, Archer." She sighed. "I have something to talk to you about. It's important."

That surprised Justice. Mae seemed happy, but was she? "Look. If you think I'm letting you go back to Black Reign just because our clubs have an alliance, think again. This is our home now. My place. My room at the club. This is home."

She sighed and put her hand over his mouth. "Would you shut up for a second?"

He rolled his eyes at her, but deep down inside, he wanted to continue protesting until she shut up.

Reaching into her back pocket, she took out a

plastic stick and handed it to him. It took Justice a moment to figure out what she was giving him. When he did, he sat down abruptly. Thank goodness there was a bench beside them. Talk about angels watching over him. If he'd landed on his ass, he'd never hear the end of it.

Mae stood there silent. Her hands were twisting together nervously. Justice took out his phone and used the flashlight, shining it on the read-out of the pregnancy test. He knew what it would be before he looked.

"I found out this morning," she said softly. "I haven't been sick or anything, but the least little thing tires me out and I've gained ten pounds in the last few weeks. I'm also eating like a fucking horse, so expect me to get bigger before I get smaller."

Justice just looked up at her, dumbfounded. Sure, he got it. But he just hadn't been expecting it. Of all the things in the world, this was the very last thing he'd thought she'd say. He opened his mouth to say something, but nothing came out.

Mae started to fidget from foot to foot, looking around them nervously. Finally, she took in a sharp breath. "Look. You don't have to do anything. Lucy and Rycks will help me with anything I need, I'm sure. I'm not asking for a commitment. I just thought you should know."

"What?" he asked sharply. "What do you mean you're not asking for a commitment?"

"We don't have to be together to have this baby. People make it work all the time. You can still be a part of our lives if you want to be."

"Fuck that shit." Justice lost all sense of control. All sense of civility. He scooped Mae up and strode to the middle of the yard.

"What are you doing? Put me down! Justice!"

"My fuckin' name is Archer! Use it!"

"What the fuck is wrong with you?" She hit at him, kicking and struggling to get down. He'd have simply tossed her over his shoulder and swatted her ass, but he didn't want to take a chance on hurting her. Instead, he gave a shrill whistle to get everyone's attention.

"Listen up! Only sayin' this once." He hefted Mae up to one shoulder, his arm clamped over her thighs to hold her in place. If she'd gained ten pounds, he couldn't tell. Her ass was narrow enough he held her easily. "This woman… is mine! Makin' her my ol' lady. Ain't got her a property patch yet, so I just want it clear who she belongs to. Also, I knocked her up. So anyone even thinks about bumpin' into her or given' her alcohol, or anything else dangerous to knocked-up females, I'll fuckin' kill ya."

Roars of laughter all around, along with slaps on his back and hollered congratulations and such. Mae wiggled until he set her down. Her little face was scrunched up disapprovingly.

"Knocked up? Really, Archer?"

He shrugged. "Sound more manly than sayin' you're pregnant."

"I'm not manly!"

"No. But I am. Seein' as how I'm the one who knocked you up."

Mae barked a laugh before finally giggling uncontrollably. "I hope someone got that on their phone. That was priceless."

Justice grinned. "Honey, I was makin' sure you knew I was keepin' you. Thought I'd made that clear before."

"With bikers, you can never tell. Not till they

make it public and put a property patch on you."

"You'll be gettin' that as soon as I can have it made. End of the week."

She ducked her head, a frown showing before she hid it. "You sure you're OK with this? You didn't seem too happy about it that first time."

"Princess, ain't nothin' gonna make me happier than you havin' my kid." He frowned then. "As long as it's a boy. Don't think havin' a girl's a good idea."

"Probably not," she agreed with a grin. "You're one step away from a caveman, and I'd hate to have to explain why all the little boys around the neighborhood are afraid to come near our house."

Justice pulled her back into his arms. "Ain't good at words, princess. But I love you."

She grinned, framing his face as she kissed him. "I love you, too, Archer." Then she gave him a worried look. "Just promise me you'll find this mole or whatever. I can't stand the thought of our children in danger because of me."

"None of this is your fault, Mae. None of it. And we'll find the rat, whoever it is. When I do, there will be no mercy." He knew he looked scary as hell, but, strangely, that seemed to comfort Mae. She smiled up at him. "Trust me?"

"I do," she said.

"Then we're in this together. I'll keep you and our kid safe, Mae. I swear it."

"I know. Now…" She grinned. "Let's go have some fun."

Marteeka Karland

Erotic romance author by night, emergency room tech/clerk by day, Marteeka Karland works really hard to drive everyone in her life completely and totally nuts. She has been creating stories from her warped imagination since she was in the third grade. Her love of writing blossomed throughout her teenage years until it developed into the totally unorthodox and irreverent style her English teachers tried so hard to rid her of.

Marteeka at Changeling: changelingpress.com/marteeka-karland-a-39

Changeling Press E-Books

More Sci-Fi, Fantasy, Paranormal, and BDSM adventures available in e-book format for immediate download at ChangelingPress.com -- Werewolves, Vampires, Dragons, Shapeshifters and more -- Erotic Tales from the edge of your imagination.

What are E-Books?

E-books, or electronic books, are books designed to be read in digital format -- on your desktop or laptop computer, notebook, tablet, Smart Phone, or any electronic e-book reader.

Where can I get Changeling Press E-Books?

Changeling Press e-books are available at ChangelingPress.com, Amazon, Apple Books, Barnes & Noble, and Kobo/Walmart.

ChangelingPress.com

Printed in Great Britain
by Amazon